Gaylord's Badge

Also by Richard Meade

BIG BEND
CARTRIDGE CREEK

Gaylord's Badge

RICHARD MEADE

F
H AM
C-2

DOUBLEDAY & COMPANY, INC.

GARDEN CITY, NEW YORK

1975

All of the characters in this book
are fictitious, and any resemblance
to actual persons, living or dead,
is purely coincidental.

First Edition
ISBN: 0-385-09952-5
Library of Congress Catalog Card Number 75-3643

AUTHOR'S NOTE

Since much of this book hinges on an election in Wyoming Territory in the early 1880s, it might be well to state that election procedures as described herein are based on contemporary accounts. Stuffed ballot boxes, indiscriminate voting by all and sundry, private ballots got up by individuals for personal gain, and all the manipulations and finaglings detailed in fictional Colter County were very much the order of the day.

Moreover, at that time Wyoming was the only state or territory granting women the right to vote; and they were active in political campaigns.

The maverick law, the abolition of the grubline, and the activities of the Knights of Labor, as well as the domination of the territory by the Stock Growers Association, eventually led to the famous Johnson County War, several years after the era in which this book is set.

Gaylord's Badge

CHAPTER I

Even in the summer, the night wind swirling down into
the basin from the peaks of the Big Horns had a touch of
chill, and Frank Gaylord, pulling on the heavy sweater,
was glad he'd brought it. A fire, of course, was out of the
question. Although it was unlikely, there was a bare
chance that the two men in the cabin down there by the
creek might spot it; and Gaylord had been a lawman for
too long to take the slightest unnecessary chance. Leaning
back against the bole of a lodgepole pine, with a big,
careful hand he even shielded the match with which he lit
perhaps the tenth cigarette of the night.

Beside him, his chief deputy, Clint Wallace, stirred rest-
lessly. "Frank, ain't it about time?"

Gaylord squinted at the silver slice of waning moon riding low over the horizon. "In a little bit," he said. "Just
have patience."

"But they're bound to be sound asleep. Have been for
hours."

"That ain't the point," Gaylord said, his deep voice pa-
tient. "Clint, I have told you this before. Always wait till
after midnight to take a sleeping man, if you can do it.
Well after midnight. Two o'clock is the best time of all. A
man's sleep is deepest then, and his mind and body both
are at their lowest point. Even when he wakes up, it takes
him longer to get himself together." He smiled faintly. "It

don't cost nothing extra to wait a little longer, and it might save a lot of trouble. Anytime you can get an edge, you take it."

Wallace made a sound in his throat. He was good, very good, Gaylord thought, but still a shade too young. Still in his late twenties, and lacking the patience that came with age, more rings on the horns. Gaylord himself would be forty on his next birthday, and patience was a lesson learned the hard way and long since absorbed into the very marrow of his bones. That was all right, though, he thought. He was slowing down a shade, and Clint was at the very peak of swiftness and alertness. Together, they made a good team.

"An edge," Clint said. "You really think Billy and Phil would resist the law?"

"Clint, we ain't paid to guess whether they will or not. We're paid to see that they don't." He paused. "Far as I know, they're both reasonable. But these warrants we're carrying could put them behind the walls for a long, long time." He drew on the cigarette, and briefly it illumined a long, craggy face: gray eyes, strong nose, a mustache with a few silver hairs among the black ones above a wide mouth with deep lines at the corners. Even hunkered down against the pine, he was a big man; erect, he was better than six feet and weighed nearly two hundred, and although he knew he had begun to drink a little more heavily lately than was his custom, so far it had put no fat on him. "Anyhow," he went on, "when a man suddenly realizes that, there's no telling what he'll do."

Clint was silent for a moment. He was as tall as Gaylord, probably would match him in bulk and muscle in due time. His face was more cleanly chiseled, a face that made the heads of all the girls in Colter County turn—what few of them there were. He had been acting sheriff when Gaylord had been invited to the county, willingly accepting demotion to chief deputy, and they had worked together now for over a year. In that time, something had sprung up between them that was deeper than the relationship between employer and employee, deeper even than friendship; almost father and son, but not quite. Call it older brother and younger one, Gaylord thought. He felt a certain apprehension stirring in him. It was good to have Clint backing him, but there were disadvantages, too. He had begun to worry about Clint's safety. Fact was that, on his own, he'd have moved in on Billy Dann and Phil Hoff by now; this edge he was so patiently taking was mostly for Clint's sake, extra insurance that Clint would not get hurt. That was a bad frame of mind for a lawman to be in about a deputy, but he had no idea what to do about it. Clint was natural-born for wearing a badge: strong, his judgment good, and, when it was necessary, fast, decisive, and accurate with a gun. And he admired Frank Gaylord extravagantly. So, for better or worse, he was probably doomed to be a law officer for a long time yet. All Gaylord could do was teach him what he needed to know to survive. And, without coddling him, expose him to no unnecessary risks while he learned.

Then Clint spat. "I still think the whole thing stinks. I've known Phil and Billy since I was a kid. Me and Billy Dann used to double up on the same horse to the schoolhouse together, down in Nebraska. They ain't no more rustlers than you or me."

"That's for the courts to decide," Gaylord said mildly. "All we know is we got warrants and we got to make arrests."

"And you know good and well who signed those war-

rants. Ross Gruber." His voice was bitter. "The Chain
Ranch."

"They're signed and certified by the district judge.
That's all that matters."

"Oh, sure. And Judge Merkel would sign a warrant
against Jesus Christ if Gruber and the Chain Ranch
asked him to." He turned to Gaylord. "Frank, tell me the
truth. Don't you agree with me? This is a damn stinkin'
frame-up. Gruber knows that Billy and Phil have been
talkin' to the Knights of Labor about organizin' a cowboy
strike this fall roundup season, and Gruber ain't about to
stand for that. So he rigged these warrants."

"Keep your voice down," Gaylord said quietly.

"All right." It dropped to a rasping whisper. "Only . . .
damn it, this sticks in my craw." He paused. "I don't
know. A lot sticks in my craw lately. Just about everything that's happening in Wyoming now, it seems like."

"The law—" Gaylord began.

"The law . . . sure. The law we're sworn to uphold. But
who makes that law, you want to know? I'll tell you.
Englishmen and Irishmen ten thousand miles away, that
have never even rode a horse across this range. Moving in
with their big cattle companies, taking up all the range,
hiring men like Gruber to manage their ranches . . . and
buying the Territorial Legislature lock, stock, and barrel.
Goddamnit, Frank, they ain't even Americans; they don't
know how Americans think. Least of all, they don't know
how a rannihan or a little rancher thinks. All they know is,
the riders that work their stock are the 'lower
classes'"—his voice was thick with mockery—"and they
figure they can treat 'em like they do their 'subjects' at
home. Work 'em when they need 'em, pay 'em what they
choose, and let 'em starve the rest of the time. And they

got this range locked up, along with half a dozen so-called Americans that think just like they do. And they just can't even understand that a man might have his own rights here, even if he don't own a foot of range or a single god-damn cow. They want it all, not just a little bit, but every ounce of it. . . ."

"Hush, Clint," Frank Gaylord said. "That ain't our problem."

"The hell it ain't. I'm sittin' out here right now, freezin' my ass off, waitin' to go down there and arrest an American friend of mine on the say-so of a manager of one of those big English spreads. And I know damned well he ain't no rustler. If he's done anything at all, it's brand his own stock. But even that's illegal now, since they've passed their damned maverick law."

Gaylord's patience was running to an end. "Clint, that's enough."

"Is it?" Clint Wallace said, and there was something strange in his voice that made Gaylord look at him; but his face was in a shadow.

Gaylord sighed. "All right, friend. Maybe it was a mistake to bring you. Maybe I should have brought Tom Callaway. But you asked to come, or did I mishear you?"

"You didn't mishear me," Clint said thinly. "I asked to come, all right. When I heard who you had to pick up, I figured I'd better. At least if I'm along they'll reach War-shield alive."

Gaylord's big hands tightened over the Winchester lying across his knees. He fought back anger. "That's a rotten thing to say."

For a moment there was only the sound of Clint's heavy

breathing. Then Wallace said, in a different voice, "Yeah, it was. I apologize, Frank. You ain't reached that point yet, I don't think."

A chill that had nothing to do with the wind from the Big Horns touched Frank Gaylord. "Clint, you'd better explain what you mean by that."

"No, I better not. I'm sorry I said it. I was out of line. Forget it, please."

Gaylord said, "It ain't the kind of thing that I'm ready to forget. I want to hear what you meant."

Clint looked at the moon. "Sure to God it's two o'clock. Let's go on down."

"Wait a minute," Gaylord answered. "We've got time for you to explain." He stood up, towering in Stetson, thick sweater, wool pants, and high-heeled boots from which spurs had been discarded lest they jingle. Clint also rose, in buckskin jacket, and shotgun chaps over blue denim. He shifted position so that his lean, intense, and handsome young face came into the moonlight.

"All right," he said. "You want me to say it, I guess I'll have to. There's talk going around, Frank. I tried to shut it out at first, but there's an awful lot of it. They say you're on the take, that Gruber and the Chain Ranch have bought you."

His voice trembled. "I didn't want to believe it at first, but everybody seems to know about it. Gruber registered a brand in your name, FTG, for Frank Tompkins Gaylord. And right now there are two hundred head of prime she-stuff wearing that brand, grazing free of charge on the Chain range." He tucked his own Winchester beneath his arm. "In today's market, that's damn near ten thousand dollars worth of beef, and the increase is worth at least a thousand a year and likely more. They say that. And that you're taking other money, too, not a lot, but some, a little at a time, from people in Warshield. And that altogether it adds up, and in the long run it's Gruber that makes it good. Oh, damn—" He struck a tree beside him with a fist. "I didn't want to bring it up. But I've been sittin' here so long, thinkin' about Billy and Phil and— Maybe it ain't so. I hope to God it ain't."

Gaylord sucked in a long breath. The barrel of the Winchester was cold beneath his hand as he ordered his thoughts. Well, it might as well be gotten over with. It, too, was part of Clint's education.

"Well, it's true," he said.

"Oh, Jesus, Frank—"

"No." Gaylord looked at the moon again; there was still time. "Suppose you hear me out; all right?"

"I'm listening," Clint said quietly.

"Good." Gaylord found it not quite comfortable to look at Clint as he spoke. Instead, he stared down the slope at the cabin in the valley, by the creek, with the big flat behind it. His mind raced back over years, many of them painful to remember. "When I come back from the Union Army, not twenty years old then, my daddy was a county sheriff in Missouri. Me, I had been through a lot, and maybe I was older than my years; anyhow, he knew I was good with guns and he swore me in as deputy. . . ."

"I've heard some of that," Clint murmured.

"And maybe you've heard what happened later. The Texas men started to bring herds up through Missouri. Those herds brought Texas fever with 'em, and they killed off every native cow anywhere they passed. Missouri laid down a deadline against Texas cattle; my daddy was enforcing it when some Texas drovers killed him. I stepped into his boots when I couldn't come close to fillin' 'em, but

I made the deadline stick, and I been in law enforcement ever since. In Missouri, in the Kansas trail towns, and now up here . . ."

"Listen, there's damned few don't know about all that." There was anguish in Clint's voice. "Everybody knows about Frank Gaylord. That's why I was so glad to step aside for you, so damned proud to serve under you. . . ."

"There's a lot they don't know about Frank Gaylord. A lot nobody knows about wearin' a badge until he's worn one as long as I have, and in as many different places." Gaylord rolled a cigarette one-handed, hardly even realizing that he did it. "What you got to understand, Clint, is that if you stay with it they'll eat you up, if you let 'em. Every town and every county's different—and yet they're all the same. They all want law and order—but not too much of it, and only for other people. And the main thing they want is that they want it cheap." He shielded the match and lit the smoke.

"They figure a lawman's like a preacher or a doctor: he's so dedicated to what he's doing, he don't need money to eat on or marry on or raise a family on. He's supposed to be glad to go out and risk his life half a dozen times a week, on call seven days out of seven, for money a store-keeper would close his place if he didn't make any more than that. But that same storekeeper will squall loudest if the commissioners vote you a ten-dollar raise; or if some-body holds him up and you don't catch him."

"Don't I know it," Clint said, with a touch of iron humor.

"You're damned well sure you know it. You've learned that much, anyhow, in the past few years." He drew in smoke, then let it out; the cabin below was dark and silent. "But what you don't understand is the reason they want to keep you broke. They want to keep you broke so they can buy you personally. If you made a decent wage, you wouldn't be for sale. . . ."

"And so the talk's right," Clint said sickly. "You're for sale now?"

"No. Only smarter. I went along for years on my salary, turning down everything they offered. And when I came here I was dead broke and pushin' forty and starting to wise up. I don't catch on very fast. But finally it dawned on me: all right, take their goddamn money. It's only what they should be paying you in salary anyhow for the work you do and the risks you take. They've made a sucker out of you for years, now you make a sucker out of them. Take anything they offer you—but don't let it make any difference. If you got to make a promise, turn the money down. But otherwise, if they don't ask and you don't promise, sock it away. It's the only way of getting paid what you're worth."

He paused. "It depends on how you run the office. If you run it so you're worth that much more than your salary, you're in the clear. If you don't, then they got their hooks in you. Me, I always run the office so they're in my debt and I can take their money with a clear conscience. It's just pay, normal salary that I would have received in the ordinary course of duty if they hadn't rigged things otherwise. It buys my best services as a lawman; it don't buy my soul, nor any special favors."

"Then—" Clint rubbed his mouth. "It's true. You have got two hundred head running on Chain range?"

"Yeah, I got those cattle there. But they're no bribe. They're a damned small payoff for a damned big service.

Remember when the Sawneys hit the bank in War-shield?"

"How could I forget? We killed Jack and Harry and two of their men."

"That's right. And if we'd been ordinary civilians we'd have collected a lot more than ten thousand in rewards. But we were lawmen in the execution of their duties. So we got nothing, even though Warshield's the only town the Sawneys never cracked. I proved right then and there that I was worth my hire; I saved the bank more than a hundred thousand dollars. Okay, the Chain Ranch's one of the biggest stockholders in the bank. If Gruber wanted to give me two hundred head of she-stock out of grati-tude, that's his business. But if he thinks it buys me, he's crazy." Gaylord paused. "You see what I'm driving at, Clint?"

"I see," Clint Wallace answered presently.

Gaylord looked at the moon, disappearing behind a butte. "The main thing is," he said, "the law. It's what you follow, like that moon yonder, that says that now it's time. It don't matter what they pay you. Nobody can buy you if you won't be bought. It's like the moon or stars. You just keep your eye on the law, and you won't get hurt."

Clint also squinted at the moon. After a while he said: "That's about all they don't control, the Wyoming Stock Growers Association out of Cheyenne. The moon and stars. But they sure have got control of the law. Frank, ain't it time to go?"

"Yeah," Gaylord said, relieved, sure that he'd explained things badly. "Like I said, it's time. There ain't no back door to the place. I'll go in first, with the carbide lamp, and you come in later and cover me. Keep to the shad-ows."

Together, guns raised, they went on foot down the slope toward the little pine-pole cabin, daubed with mud, by the swift, narrow creek.

———————————

Billy Dann and Phil Hoff, who had jointly homesteaded quarter sections, had laid a footbridge across the little stream. Gaylord ran over it, crouched, rifle in his right hand, carbide lamp in his left, Clint just behind. They fetched up beside the blank side wall of the cabin. There Gaylord raised the shield and lit the carbide lamp. When, hissing, it sent out its white light, he dodged around the corner. "Open in the name of the law!" he yelled, and at the same time kicked wide the unlatched door and sprang into the cabin.

The lamp's glare raked over a pair of rough bunks along the far wall. In the bottom one, a man in long johns raised his head, opening bleary eyes. In the top, under a worn blanket, a naked man rolled over, propped up on one elbow, and grunted, "Whah?" Then both squinted into the blinding light. Neither was any older than Clint Wallace, despite the long beard Billy Dann, the man in underwear, wore.

Dann blinked and shook his head as Clint Wallace came in the door behind Gaylord. "What the hell?" Dann mumbled.

"Frank Gaylord, Billy. You and Phil stand fast and don't make a break. I've got warrants to serve on both of you. You're under arrest."

"Arrest?" Phil Hoff sat up, blanket falling away from his skinny torso. He rubbed his face, blinded by the carbide glare. "Gaylord?" Then: "Clint. Boy, what in fire is this all about?"

"Warrants for rustling, Phil," Clint said tautly. "You and Billy are being taken in for rustling."

There was, then, save for the hissing of the lamp, total silence in the cabin as the two awakening men tried to grapple with this news.

After a minute Billy Dann let out a breath and swung out of bed, tousled hair and beard in points. As his dirty feet hit the floor he squinted at Wallace. "Clint, what kind of warrants? Who signed 'em?"

"Chain," Wallace answered. "Gruber."

"Ah." In the bunk above, Phil Hoff breathed an obscenity. "Might have knowed. Clint, this is a pile of crap."

"I know that, too, Phil," Clint said wearily. "But we got to take you in. Judge issued these warrants and they're valid." His voice was almost pleading. "You know me and Frank. It ain't our doing. It's just our job. Now, for God's sake, come with us quietly."

Dann stood up and Gaylord watched him narrowly as he drew on old canvas pants, a hole in one knee. "Well, don't shoot me," he said. "I got to have some coffee. Lemme stir up the fire. There's half a pot left from supper."

"Go ahead, Billy," Gaylord said. He had inventoried guns now. Their Colts and pistol belts hung on chairs; their rifles were in the corner. "I could use some myself."

Leaving the carbide lamp burning, he lit the kerosene lantern hanging from a ceiling pole. Hoff, in the upper bunk, began to curse, slowly, steadily. "Rustlin'. Rustlin', my ass! We ain't rustled no Chain steers, nobody's cows."

"Gruber alleges you branded mavericks outside the regular association roundup."

Hoff rolled over. "We branded nothin' but the increase

from our own hundred head on our own land! What's wrong with that?"

"It's against the law," Clint Wallace said dully. "All brandin's done at the association roundup. The maverick law," he added bitterly.

"Maverick law!" Billy Dann turned, blue enamel coffeepot in hand. "A law the big dogs rammed through so they can take all the unbranded cattle on the range, save them that walks beside their mamas! What kind of law is it says every maverick in this district has to be put into a pool and sold to the highest bidder for the benefit of the Stock Growers Association in Cheyenne? And a man's got to post a three-thousand-dollar bond before he can even bid! It's nothin' but a dodge to take our own cattle away from us, like the law that says nobody can hold a roundup except under association authority." He spat on the dirt floor of the cabin. "Everybody knows it's unconstitutional. Ain't worth a damn, except for the rich to rob the poor."

"Billy, we can't help that," Clint said. "We got to enforce it."

"Oh, sure, sure." Hoff had grabbed the bottom of a pair of long johns and pulled them on. He dropped from the top bunk and sat on the lower one, running a hand through tousled hair. "Anyhow, it ain't the mavericks, and you know it. That ain't why Gruber sent you after us."

"I think there's been enough palaver," Gaylord said. "Phil, git some clothes on." He picked up the pistol belts and tossed them into the far corner.

Hoff's face contorted. "Maybe you can lay the law on us, but you can't shut our mouths. It's because we're tryin' to get the cowboys on this range to strike. They been crapped on too long by these English spreads. Worked for bottom wages when they're needed, turned loose to starve in the winter, not even welcome ridin' the grubline through the off season anymore. You come onto one of them big ranches now, and they give you one meal and roust you. And time was when any man was welcome to stay two weeks, maybe longer, at any spread. . . . And if you complain or cause any trouble, the association black-lists you all over Wyomin' so you can't work anywhere in the territory. . . . They figure they got us all by the short hair and they can treat us any way they want to . . . especially Gruber. He's worse than an English lord himself, and he's American!"

"I said get your clothes on," Gaylord snapped. "You can have your say in court."

"Court." Billy Dann set down the coffeepot and clipped off the single word so that it rang like iron. It was as if the full realization had just struck home. "We got to go to court, stand trial, lawyers and all that?"

"Yes," Gaylord said. Wanting a cigarette, he knew better than to relax. They were coming fully awake now. "Yeah, that's the way it is, Billy."

"And if we're convicted what do we get?" Phil Hoff asked, still sitting on the bunk's edge.

"Two to five years in Rawlins, likely," Clint said with a profound bitterness.

"Two to five—" Billy Dann's voice broke. He stared at Clint, then turned to Gaylord. "Frank, for God's sake. You know us better than that. I swear we never branded no stock but our own. You wouldn't take us in and put us behind the walls for that long, would you?"

Gaylord shook his head. He had a knack, which he used now. Keep your eye on the law, he'd told Clint. Watch it like the moon, the stars. Mentally, emotionally, he did that, blanking out all human response to the pleading in Dann's voice. "I got no option."

"You got one. You got a good one. You came after us and we wasn't here. We'd done hauled freight; you never seen us. Frank, Clint, for cryin' out loud . . . five years in the *pen*? Listen, we'll ride out as fast as we can get dressed and saddled. Clear the district, and that ought to satisfy Ross Gruber."

"Frank," Clint Wallace said softly, "I kind of think that's the way it was. The birds had done flown the cage. . . ."

Gaylord sucked in a long breath. "No, it won't work. We got to take 'em in."

"Frank—"

"Clint, you know better than that. These are legal warrants and we got to serve 'em."

Wallace looked from Hoff to Dann to Gaylord. "Well—" he said sickly.

Dann spat again. "So that's it, huh, Clint? I knowed Gaylord had sold out to Gruber. Everybody knows it. But you too, huh? How many head is Gruber runnin' free for you?"

"Billy—" Clint's face twisted.

"It's one way to git rich quick, I reckon." Dann turned back to the stove, then knocked over the coffeepot. It fell, spilling brown liquid. "Hell—"

Instinctively Gaylord's head jerked around. At that instant Dann yelled, "Phil!" He threw himself sideways, and simultaneously Hoff's hand slid under the pine-needle pillow on the bottom bunk and came up with a short-nosed Colt, lined on Gaylord.

"Frank!" Clint Wallace bawled, and Gaylord jumped aside as the revolver went off. Hard on its deep cough came the short, flat bark of Wallace's rifle. Both sounds were terrific in the little cabin, seeming to jar the walls. Even as guns thundered, Gaylord swung his Winchester, clubbing Billy Dann hard across the temple before the man's hand could close on a poker.

Gaylord felt the shock up through his wrists. Dann pitched forward, landing hard. Gaylord whirled.

Phil Hoff lay slumped back on the bunk, eyes wide open, staring, naked breast spouting red. He opened his mouth and blood trickled out. "Clint," he said, a gurgling sound. "Clint, Jesus." Then he died, eyes still open, body unmoving; and suddenly it was over.

Clint Wallace lowered the Winchester, a wisp of smoke still curling from its barrel. In the carbide glare, his face was white as paper.

"Well," he whispered. "Well." He stared at Gaylord strangely and his mouth opened and closed, but no words came out. His eyes shuttled to Billy Dann, lying face down on the hard-packed floor. Then Clint lurched to the door, leaned out, and vomited into the cool, clean night.

Gaylord started toward him, then halted. Instead, he busied himself putting handcuffs on the unconscious Billy Dann. As he straightened up, Clint pulled back inside the cabin, wiping his mouth. His eyes were wide, wild, as he looked at Gaylord. His hand shook as it went to the star pinned on his jacket. He ripped off the badge and hurled it across the room. It hit the stove with a tiny clink and bounced away.

"All right, Frank," Clint whispered, and there was fury in the sound. "There it is. I'm through. Pick up your stinking badge and carry it to Gruber like a dog with a bone in its mouth." He hit the doorjamb brutally with one bare fist and then almost ran out into the darkness.

The room stank of powdersmoke, blood, and the dead

man's involuntary excretions. Gaylord stood motionless, and he neither tried to stop Clint nor call to him.

Curiously, when he turned back to Dann, who was beginning to groan and stir, all he felt was a profound relief.

CHAPTER II

"It was a mistake," said Gaylord. "I shoulda taken another deputy, not Clint. If he hadn't counted on Clint's friendship, Phil Hoff would never have dared make that break." He poured himself another drink.

"That's three," Carla Doane said, an edge to her usually soft, husky voice. "And it's not even dinnertime yet. You never used to drink in the morning, Frank."

He looked at her, the tall, handsome, dark-haired woman in her thirties, at whose kitchen table he now sat. For privacy, the blinds were drawn; but both of them knew that it was an open secret in the town that they had been lovers for the past year. A fine woman, he thought, the most woman he had ever met or known in his whole life—but she did have a knack of putting her finger on your sore spots sometimes. A touch defensively he said, "It's not mornin' for me. Don't forget I've been up all night. Besides"—he sipped the whiskey—"when your chief deputy's had to kill a man in an arrest, and then he throws the badge square in your teeth, it shakes you up."

Carla nodded, not without sympathy. "I suppose."

"I tried to talk to him," Gaylord said. "He was down in the creekbottom, in that little house that dance-hall girl lives in."

"You mean Joey Moore." Taking a coffee cup from the shelf, Carla went to the stove. Full-bosomed, slender-waisted, and long of leg, she moved with a thoroughbred's easy grace, Gaylord thought admiringly.

"Yeah, that's her. I knocked and she let me in. Then she went in the other room, so we could talk. Only"—he sighed—"there wasn't much talkin' I could do. I tried to tell him not to take it so hard, just take time off, a leave of absence, somethin'. Maybe go back to Nebraska to see his folks a spell. Then, when he come back, his badge would be here waitin' for him. But he just looked at me and laughed. And"—he drank—"it ain't the kind of laugh I ever want to hear again."

"I'm sorry." Carla, with her coffee, sat down across the table from him.

"No more badge for him," Gaylord continued tautly. "He'd already figured it out, on the way back here to Warshield. He was through with lawin'—forever. He'd already asked that dance-hall girl to marry him, and she'd said yes. And now he's got it figured that he's gonna take up a homestead right next to Billy Dann's. Maybe buy Billy's, too, if they put him away in Rawlins."

"Which they will likely do," said Carla bitterly.

Gaylord did not answer that. He drained the glass and, avoiding Carla's eyes, reached for the bottle one more time. "In a way, when I heard that, I'm kind of glad it worked out like that. To tell the truth, it ain't a good idea for a sheriff to like one of his deputies much as I like Clint. When a lawman's in a tight spot, he can't let worryin' about one of his men gittin' hurt slow him down. But I'd started doin' that with Clint—hesitatin', freezin' up just a little in a clinch, takin' a risk of botchin' things for his sake. That could get us both killed someday. Anyhow, that little girl will make him a good wife, no matter that she's come up a rough way, and he can go to ranchin' and live to a ripe old age."

"You think so?" Carla's mouth twisted. "What makes you think he'll be that lucky? Dann, Hoff, every other small rancher who's tried to get a start near Chain—one way or the other, Ross Gruber's found a way to destroy all of them. What's to stop Clint from being next?"

"Me," said Gaylord.

"You?"

"I'll talk to Gruber. I'll tell him to keep his hands off Clint. I'll make sure the boy gets a fair chance."

"I see." She looked down at her coffee. "So that's the way it works, eh? If the sheriff's on your side, you're okay. Otherwise, you may die in your bunk at two in the morning, like poor Phil Hoff."

Something tightened in Gaylord's chest. He scraped back his chair and rose. "Woman, what's got into you?"

"I think you know." Carla stood up, dark eyes huge in a face gone pale. "I'm scared, Frank. Afraid for you."

"That's craziness."

"Is it? I hope so. But . . . those two hundred head Gruber gave you. The free meals and room at Garrison's Hotel, the whiskey on the house and—they say—a little rake-off from the games at Clanton's gambling house . . ."

Gaylord sucked in breath. "That amounts to nothin', absolutely nothin'. Sure, Garrison puts me up free; Clanton buys my drinks. And, yeah, if I'm off duty he pays me for spending time there, keepin' order. . . ."

"You're never off duty and the county pays you for keeping order, Frank. Like Gruber's cattle . . . they're bribes, Frank; nothing else."

"No—" Gaylord began, but she cut him off.

"Maybe you can't see it, but everybody else can. Look, Garrison's speculating in town lots and cutting corners doing it. Clanton's games, they say, are none too straight. And everybody knows about Gruber. Now, if the time comes and citizens complain, will you move against those people the way you moved against Phil Hoff and Billy Dann? Or will you draw back a little—"

"I'll move against anybody who breaks the law," said Gaylord harshly.

She looked at him for a moment, long and hard. "Yes," she said at last. "I guess you mean that . . . now. But I can't help remembering what happened to Lin." She paused; her voice was soft when she went on: "When we were married, he was the most respected lawyer in Denver, absolutely honest, and I was proud to be his wife. Then the association hired him and brought us to Cheyenne, and he fell under the influence of men like Gruber. And I saw it happen—the fat fees, the power, the political future they dangled in front of him. It got into his system just like poison. Oh, he didn't *think* he was selling out, not at first. But he did, bit by bit, one little piece of his soul at a time. And then he had nothing else left to sell. He suddenly realized that when the big ranchers rigged a case against a man they wanted hanged—and demanded that Lin be special prosecutor. Then he had to make a choice. Either break with them, or push it through, knowing the whole thing was a frame-up. Well, he won his case; and they were proud of him. And two hours after the man was hanged, he shot himself."

"I'm not Linwood Doane," said Gaylord thickly.

"No. And I don't want to take the chance of your becoming a Linwood Doane." She came to him then, hands on his arms, looking up at him, pleading. "Frank, listen.

Don't run for reelection this fall! Let's leave Colter
County, leave Wyoming. Get a job somewhere else, where
you don't have all these dirty pressures. I don't care where,
I'll go anywhere with you! But give Gruber and the others
their badge back! It's just not worth it."

Gaylord looked down at her, fighting his own emotions.
There was almost nothing he would not do for her, but
she was asking the impossible. "No," he said.

She stepped back. "Why not?"

Carefully Frank Gaylord sought his words. "First place,
I'm a lawman, nothing else; and lawman's jobs are hard to
find these days. The country's taming down; there ain't
the call there used to be for men to walk into a tough
place and jerk a knot in its tail. Oh, I might get on as a
town marshal somewhere, or on the police in Denver, but
I couldn't break into a new county and run for sheriff and
expect to get elected. It takes a long time to build up the
rep and connections a man's got to have for that. But I've
got all that set here in Colter County, and I'm a cinch for
reelection."

"That's what scares me."

He felt the scrape of anger, made rawer by the whiskey. "I can't help that!" He whipped a bankbook from his
vest pocket and threw it on the table. "Look there. Seven
hundred dollars in my account, and it's all I got to show
for years of work and risk. That look to you like a crooked
sheriff gettin' fat off of graft? After four years in office
here, you think there couldn't be ten, twenty times that
much in there if I'd played it the way you seem to think
I have?"

He paused. "Why do you think I never asked you to
marry me? You think I don't love you, wouldn't be proud
to have you for my wife? Well, I'll tell you why. Because I

got nothin' to give you, no right to ask any woman to marry me like things stand!"

She opened her mouth to speak, but he rushed on. "So, yeah, I let Gruber give me cattle, Garrison give me free room and board, Clanton a drink or two and a little cash. For what I've done for this town and county, I'm entitled to have a chance to build up a stake, enough so I can have a decent life. Well, I've got a stake now—those cattle out at Chain. And before you start tellin' me to give 'em back, I'll say this: They're what make the difference. With my brand on those, I can do what I've never had the right to do before—ask you to marry me."

"Frank—" She said the one word and could not go on.

"That's it, Carla. I'm proposing to you, here and now. What about it? Will you say yes? Or would you rather I tear up Gruber's bill of sale and we keep on the way we're goin'—sneakin' around behind pulled curtains, with the whole town snickerin' behind our backs?"

"Frank," she said again and turned away. Then she said hoarsely, "You big fool, it's not the money. I don't care about the money. I've got plenty of it—"

"Linwood's money. No, thanks, ma'am. I've got my own pride, strange as that may seem to you."

She turned. "Darling, I didn't mean . . ."

"Maybe not. But I can't help it. It's the way I feel." He picked up his glass, drained it. "I'm not sellin' my soul bit by bit, no matter what you think. I'm not takin' a penny more than I've really earned. Listen, you think I'm a fool? I know these people will use you if you give 'em a chance. But so do the others, the ones that say they got no ax to grind. They want you to risk your life to keep 'em safe, but they don't want to pay you enough to live on, much

less marry or have anything for your kids or your old age.
Well, I'm not gonna be used by either side. I'm gonna do
my duty like I swore to, regardless of who it hurts, and no
matter what they give me, it don't buy a piece of me, not
a hair!" He picked up the bankbook. "All I'm askin' is that
you trust me, have a little confidence in me. And . . . I'm
waitin' for your answer."

Carla drew in a breath that made her breasts rise beneath her blouse. She did not look at him. "I can't give
you one right now."

"Why not?"

She turned. "Because a burnt child dreads the fire. I've
been through it once and I'll not go through it again. I
. . . Frank, let's wait and see."

Something seemed to collapse inside him. He felt old,
tired, heavy. "You mean wait and see whether I sell out or
not."

Carla did not answer.

Gaylord slipped the bankbook into his pocket. "Okay,"
he said. "Maybe it was all wrong anyway. It's one thing to
trust a man enough to sleep with him, I reckon, and
another to trust him enough to marry him." He wanted to
say more but his pride clogged his throat, and he strode to
the back door. "Okay, we'll let things ride," he managed.

She made a helpless, silent gesture. Gaylord opened the
door, went out, and closed the door behind him.

———————◆———————

Dust, borne by the ceaseless wind, swirled down the
wide main street of Warshield. On the sidewalk, Gaylord
clamped his hat down tighter. This town had not even
existed fifteen years ago. Then the Sioux, Cheyennes, and
Crows had held this section of Wyoming. But the coming

of the railroad and the great cattle explosion out of Texas
had doomed the Indians; Little Big Horn had been the
high-water mark of their resistance. Now, eight years
later, they starved on reservations; the buffalo were gone;
and this fine range country was jammed, pressed down,
and running over with cattle. It was like another gold
rush—the beef bonanza, some people called it.

Gaylord nodded to the people he passed; everyone
here, of course, knew him. He passed his office and kept
on going, bound for Clanton's House of Chance. What
Carla did not understand, he told himself, was that there
was no way a law officer could be paid enough to hold
down a county like Colter. Right now Wyoming was the
hot spot of the West, and Colter was the hot spot of
Wyoming.

That was because word of the enormous fortunes to be
made in beef had reached the East and Europe, and the
big-money people there had flared their nostrils like
wolves scenting meat. They had poured capital into the
territory, staggering amounts; in fact, they had damned
near bought the place outright. Now Wyoming was dominated by great ranches owned by absentee companies and
syndicates, many British, usually with actual management
vested in Americans, though there were huge spreads
owned by natives, too. Anyhow, all those cattle barons
had one thing in common—a determination to wrench
every nickel of profit possible from this range.

As Clint had said, they owned the Territorial Legislature through their Cheyenne-based association and they
made the laws to suit themselves: laws designed to
squeeze out competition, wipe out what small spreads
there were, and make sure no others got a start. On top of
that, they had cut cowboys' wages, and wiped out the

time-honored privilege of grubline riding, which enabled
jobless punchers to winter over until work became avail-
able in spring; they treated cowhands as if they were em-
ployees in some shoe factory back East or a cotton mill in
England. And, of course, such men would not take that
kind of oppression lying down. The small ranchers cut
wire and mavericked to stay alive; the cowboys talked
about forming a union and calling a strike at roundup
time. Gaylord paused and rolled a cigarette. What Carla
did not understand was that the time was drawing near
when only a strong sheriff, exerting all his power, could
prevent war between the big ranchers and the small ones
and the cowboys. The wind that swept down this street
was tainted now with dust; it was Gaylord's duty to keep
it from reeking of blood. Warshield, with its two streets
and its scatter of frame-and-brick buildings, was not, at
this moment, a town at all: it was a powderkeg.

And she wanted him to turn loose, hightail out and
dodge the biggest challenge of his career, and leave the
county—*his* county—to a lesser man.

Well, he would not do it. Let her, let anyone, think
what they wanted to: he knew Frank Tompkins Gaylord,
and he knew that he could not be bought by anybody. All
right, so Clint was gone, Hoff dead, Dann in jail, and
Carla thought he was a weak sister like her first husband.
They would see—and so would Gruber, if he got crosswise of the law.

What they did not understand was Gaylord's rule, the
star he always guided on: No one was above the law.

Now he had reached Clanton's. Well, he would have
one drink there and get the business he had with Clanton
over with. Tom Callaway had the duty and, though not as
good a deputy as Clint, he was a competent man. After

he'd finished with Clanton, Gaylord told himself, he would go back to Garrison's Hotel and sleep for six hours. Maybe things would look better then.

———————

"One more, Sheriff," Clanton said.

"No, thanks, Sam. I've had my bait."

They were sitting in a corner of the front barroom, at Clanton's private table. The owner of the saloon and gambling hall was short, stocky, and as pale as a mushroom, in gray suit and starched linen. Because he dealt in his own games, his nails were neatly trimmed. "Suit yourself." He raised his own glass. "*Salud y pesetas.*"

"Same to you." Frank Gaylord drank, then set down his glass. "Sam, I got to tell you something."

Clanton's pale eyes brightened. "Shoot."

"I've been thinkin'." Gaylord tried to phrase it diplomatically. "I've heard talk, and I hate to say it, but this off-duty deal we got goin' is finished. It don't look good for me to be in here at nights as much as I've been. You better hire a private guard from now on. It's not proper for the sheriff to lend his personal protection to a gamblin' joint."

Promptly Clanton smiled. "Well, I'm glad you finally realized that."

Gaylord sat up straight. "You are?"

"Sure. Hell, I told you to start with, what I was really after was to make sure you were happy in Colter County. All I aimed for was to make sure you'd stay on and run for reelection, even if those chinch-bugs on the county board won't raise your salary. I never meant for you to be around here all the time, the way you've been, so damned determined to make sure you earn every penny that you get." He grinned. "Tell the truth, it's bad for business havin' the sheriff in here so much; makes me look like I'm bein' watched especially close. So if you don't come around as much in the future, hell, I'll understand—though we'll always be glad to see you."

"Wait a minute," Gaylord said. "I don't think you understand. What I'm sayin' is that I don't want any more money from you. The whole deal's off, that fifty a month included."

"Aw, come on, Frank." Clanton leaned back, still smiling. "You're the one that's missed the point." Then he was grave. "Hell, man, you know me well enough to know that I don't throw money away. And I'm saying that I want to keep on paying that fifty whether you come around or not." His eyes were like chips of ice. "Listen, I remember what this town was like BG—before Gaylord. Clint was okay, but he was too young and lightweight for the job. Fights in here every night, the breakage as much in a week as I'm givin' you a month . . . You eliminated all that, chased out the wild bunch, and now we've got law and order, and I make money out of law and order. So, if you don't mind, I'd like to keep up the monthly payment whether you come around or not. No obligation; I'll never ask you for a favor. Call it a campaign contribution if you want to. All I know is, we can't afford to lose you. So if we got to subsidize you, we'll do it."

Gaylord was flattered and pleased by the sincerity of the man; moreover, he knew that everything Clanton said was true. Nevertheless, there was Carla. "Sam, I can't—"

"Hush," Clanton said. "Yes, you can." His hand moved beneath the table, then he leaned forward, gripped Gaylord's hand, and dropped coins into the palm. "That's for this month, and it ain't fifty, it's sixty, three double eagles.

And don't give me any crap about not takin' it. Not when
the board only pays you seventy-five a month and fees,
and you got your jail to run and deputies to hire. This is
Clanton's contribution to the best law enforcement money
can buy—no more, no less."

The gold was heavy in Gaylord's palm. He thought of
Carla. Something had gone wrong somewhere. But it was
money he needed and money he had earned, and would
keep on earning if someone didn't kill him while he did
his work. Somehow he could not return it, all that sweetly
heavy coin. "You understand this buys no special favors,"
he said hoarsely as he put it into his pocket.

"Have I ever asked for any?"

"No," said Gaylord.

"Then there's your answer."

The sixty dollars would go straight into the bank account. "As long as that's understood," Gaylord said. "Well
. . ." He shoved back his chair. But as he rose the front
door opened, and Ross Gruber entered, followed by his
bodyguard.

CHAPTER III

Chain. Ross Gruber was Chain Ranch, and Chain Ranch was Warshield, and so you could say that Ross Gruber was the town and maybe even Colter County, half of which Chain Ranch owned. Chain Ranch's patronage supported its merchants; Chain's taxes paid Gaylord's base salary; and it was Chain's cowboys who would reelect him this year.

Chain Ranch was money and it was power, and all that seemed concentrated in the broad-shouldered, stocky figure of Ross Gruber, who, seeing Gaylord at the table, came to him.

Gruber was a cowman, and there were few better in the territory. But the hat cocked on his head was that of a Union Cavalry major, which he had been in the Civil War, and he wore boiled shirt, store suit, and tie with diamond stickpin. Face a sunburned square, with broken nose, hard black eyes, small mouth, and craggy chin, he walked with a military bearing acquired at West Point. The gun on his hip was a new Colt Peacemaker, in a flapped military holster. He had stayed in the Army after the war and had been a military attaché at the Court of St. James, where he had made his connection with the English owners of Chain.

He strode briskly to the table and Clanton stood up. For

a moment Gaylord thought he might even bow. He himself said only, "Hello, Major."

"Frank." Gruber put out a thick-fingered hand. His voice was deep and brisk, his grip strong. Then, more perfunctorily, he greeted Clanton. "Sam, I'd like to talk privately to Frank. Send over my special scotch, will you?"

"Yes, sir." Clanton scurried off.

Gruber took his chair. Behind him, his two men, Lang and Withers, remained standing. Both wore Colts, and there was no law against that, but Lang carried a sawed-off shotgun under one arm. Gaylord said, "Lang, you'll have to check that gun."

Lang's face reminded Gaylord of a skull he had once seen, with the meat still on it, that had fallen off of a Crow burial platform. "Well . . ."

"Check the shotgun," Gruber said commandingly.

"Yes, sir." Lang turned to deposit it with the bartender.

A waiter came with whiskey. Gruber had a shot poured into Gaylord's glass, then his own, and the bottle was left on the table. "Frank," Gruber said, "the news just reached me. I congratulate you."

"On what?"

"Eliminating that rustler Hoff. And bringing in his partner."

Gaylord felt a kind of chill. "You got the wrong man. It's Clint Wallace that killed Hoff."

"Then, by damn, I'll have a talk with Wallace and show him my appreciation."

Gaylord sniffed the exotic, smoky-smelling whiskey. "I don't think he'll stand still for being appreciated, Major. He shot because Hoff was reaching for a gun to resist arrest."

"So? Main thing is, Hoff's dead, Dann's bound for

prison, two troublemakers gone. Both were active in the Knights of Labor, you know, the outfit that's trying to organize the cowboys."

"That don't matter to Clint. Dann and Hoff were his friends."

"Of course, of course, And he's bound to be low. Nobody likes to kill a man unless there's something wrong with him. But we need a man like him in law enforcement here."

"He ain't in law enforcement no more," Gaylord said; and he told Gruber about Clint. "He threw his badge in my face. He's going to marry up and claim some range next to Dann's."

"Oh," said Gruber, and it was as if shades were pulled down over his eyes. "Oh, now, that would be a mistake."

Frank Gaylord was exhausted, more than a little drunk, and he said harshly, "No, it ain't no mistake. The land is open for settlement. Clint's takin' it up, and maybe he'll buy Dann's spread in due time, too. There is no law whatsoever against him startin' a ranch there."

"Why there is," said Gruber. "The maverick law. All these little ranchers brand anything they see without an iron—"

"So do the big ones," Gaylord said.

"No, we don't. Under the new law, all mavericks are put into a pool and stockmen bid them in for the benefit of the association."

"Which freezes out the little men," Gaylord said. "What it really is is a law to let the big ranchers acquire all the mavericks on the range."

"Frank," Gruber said, "I don't like to hear you talking like that."

Gaylord was very tired and had drunk too much.

Carla's pale face and enormous eyes swam momentarily in
his vision. "Major, I don't care how you like to hear me
talk," he said tiredly. "Clint killed a man last night and
resigned, and that hurt me worse than anything has since
God knows when. I ain't concerned about you right now,
I'm concerned about Clint."

"Now, wait a minute," said Gruber, and he drank some
scotch. Lang came back from the bar and took up station
behind him. Then Gruber said, "Of course, I'm concerned
about Wallace, too. He was a good lawman in his time,
and I expect he'll make a good cattleman. And he did kill
Hoff, which, God knows, was a public service. Sure, he's
upset about it. But . . . maybe fifty head of two-year-olds
will ease his hurt and express our gratitude."

"What?" Gaylord said.

"Chain would like to give Clint Wallace fifty head of
young beef to express our gratitude for killing Hoff."

Gaylord said harshly, "He wouldn't take 'em. Hoff was
his friend—and he hates Chain."

"All the more reason why we should try to change his
attitude." Gruber poured another drink. "But I guess
you're right, Frank. He'd get the wrong idea if we made
the offer. Still, I think he ought to have the cattle. Why
don't you give 'em to him?"

"Me?"

Gruber said, "Lang, bring me pen, ink, and some
paper."

"Yes, sir." The tall, skull-faced gunman strode off.

"I think I don't understand," said Gaylord.

"Just wait, Frank," Gruber said, and poured Gaylord's
glass full.

Lang came back with the paper, ink, and pen, and

Gruber immediately began to write. He passed a sheet to Gaylord. "There. A bill of sale from Chain for sixty two-year-olds to your brand."

Gaylord stared at it. "Sixty two-year-olds . . ."

"Fifty to replace the fifty you will personally give young Wallace," Gruber said. "We do want to see him get ahead. And ten more for yourself, as a token of our appreciation for your part in the Dann-Hoff matter. When Wallace is settled in, our riders will deliver the fifty head as a gift from you. Meanwhile, you've got two hundred ten head, plus the increase, still grazing on Chain range."

"Now, wait a minute," Gaylord said.

"Look, Frank, let's not argue about it, all right?" Gruber raised a hand. "Chain pays its debts—to you, to Wallace, to anyone it feels it owes. Besides, I don't have time to go into a lot of discussion. The stage from Cheyenne is due in ten minutes from now, and that's why I'm in town. My sister's on it. Florence. Her first trip West. Anyhow, there's the bill of sale. Keep the cattle or give 'em to Wallace, it's entirely up to you." He stood up. "Now, come along with us. I want you to meet Florence. She's really a charming person, even if she is"—he laughed hoarsely—"sister to an old boar hog like me."

Gaylord sat there for a moment, looking at the bill of sale. Then he put it into his pocket. Yes, by God, Clint deserved it, that much start. And while he wouldn't take it from Chain, he wouldn't turn down such a gift from Frank Gaylord.

Gaylord tucked the paper into his vest. Then he rose. "All right, I'll go along with you."

"Good. I want Florence to meet the best element here right away."

He had had too much to drink, Gaylord knew as he followed Gruber and his two bodyguards toward the door. He was not quite steady on his feet, and his eyes felt as if someone had rubbed tobacco in them, hard. His nerves were tautly strung, and he was dead for sleep. All sorts of emotional currents swirled in him. And that was why, when someone at the bar yelled his name hoarsely and he spun, his hand was already on the butt of his pistol.

"Who—?" he said, his eyes searching the men ranged along the counter. Then one detached himself, hands high. He was as tall as Gaylord himself, with great, sloping shoulders, narrow waist, and rider's hairpin legs; his garb was shabby range clothes, his Stetson battered and grease-stained, his shirt dirty, tattered, his jeans faded, out at the knee, his boot heels run over into little knobby balls.

"Gaylord," this man said. "Proud of yourself?"

"Friend," Gaylord said, "I don't know—"

"Sho you don't," the man said. His face was a sunburned wedge, his eyes cool hazel, his chin strong; he was about thirty-five, Gaylord judged. "So I'll introduce myself. My name's Lew Morrell, from Texas. And you can let go that gun, big man. I ain't heeled."

Gaylord's eyes flashed to his waist and saw the truth of that. Morrell wore no gun. He let his own hand slip from the Colt butt. "All right. You got business with me?"

"Just to say congratulations," Morrell answered. "Hear you took care of a pair of real bad hombres last night. Worst goddamn pair since the Sam Bass gang."

"Morrell . . . you ain't makin' sense."

Morrell straightened up. "Well, it don't make no sense to kill honest cowboys like they were outlaws." His voice was hard, and his eyes harder. "Only a goddamn carrion-eatin' coyote would be proud of that."

Frank Gaylord felt blood mounting to his face. "Morrell—"

"That's right, you run me in. You can cook up some charge, you ass-kissin' tin badge. You and the association always can against anybody that bucks you. . . ." He spat on the floor. "You want to know somethin', Sheriff Gaylord? You make a goddamn sheepdog look like George Washington when it comes to independence. Well, you ain't goin' to have it your way forever, you and Chain—"

Lang stepped forward. "Morrell." His hands dangled at his hips; his skull face was pale. "You leave Chain out of this."

"You a deputy?" Morrell jeered. "No, just a professional killer. Comes to the same thing in this county." Then he turned his back on all of them. "Johnny, give me another whiskey. Got to have somethin' to settle my stomach."

The contempt in that gesture roused rage in Gaylord, but when Lang moved forward again he threw out his arm. "Leave him be!" he snapped.

"You heard what he said about Chain!"

Gruber's voice was soft. "Ease off, Lang. It's a free country, and anyhow he's not armed. That's a favorite tactic, incidentally, of the organizers of the Knights of Labor—not carrying guns." He turned away; at that moment there was whooping on the street. "The stage is coming in, with my sister on it. Let's go."

But Gaylord stood there, staring at Morrell's back. He felt mingled rage and shame and a need to confront this

man, learn who he really was and why he was in Warshield. Then Gruber took his arm. "Come on, Frank."

———————————

The six-up hitch traveled at a trot between stations, but
it always broke into a run coming into town. Ferd
Shoffner, the driver, let out a yodeling call to announce
his arrival, then checked the sweating team. With jingle
of harness and creak of leather thoroughbraces, the Con-
cord skidded to a stop before the office of the transit company.

Then Ferd had jumped down and was opening the
doors. "Warshield! Two hours here! Everybody out for
Warshield!"

Standing beside Gruber, Frank Gaylord waited as Ferd
opened the coach door. Then Gruber made a sound in his
throat and stepped forward. At the same time, a kind of
sigh arose from the crowd that had gathered to meet the
coach and collect their mail. It was a tribute to the
woman who, pausing on the step, looked around, saw
Gruber, and cried out: "Ross!"

"Florence, my dear." Gruber put out his hand.

Taking it, she stepped down, target for every eye in the
crowd, including Gaylord's. Blond, with fine blue eyes,
ivory skin, cleanly chiseled nose, small, red mouth, she
wore a blue traveling dress that dramatized her coloring
and hugged her figure: full breasts, slender waist, curved
hips. Gaylord even caught a glimpse of dainty ankle as
she stepped down. A hell of a good-looking girl, he
thought. Maybe twenty-three, twenty-four at the most.

She and Gruber hugged and kissed, trading words lost
in the noise of the crowd. She stepped back and laughed,
showing teeth white and perfect. Gruber spoke again and

he and his sister turned, and then Gaylord realized with some confusion that he was about to be presented to her. "Sheriff Frank Gaylord, my sister Florence Gruber."

"Delighted, Sheriff Gaylord." Her small, gloved hand took his big one. "Ross has mentioned you in his letters."

Gaylord swept off his hat. "Pleased to meet you, Miss Gruber."

"You must come to see us at Chain Ranch," she said. "I'm eager to meet all of Ross's western friends."

"That's right, Frank. I'm having a gala dinner up at Chain to introduce Florence to the folks around here, next Saturday night. Be sure to come, around five. Be a lot of people there you ought to meet anyhow. Okay?"

"I—" Gaylord hesitated. "I'll be there."

"I'll be looking for you." The girl smiled and withdrew her hand. Then, as she turned away, somebody behind Gaylord gave a long, drawn-out, suggestive whistle.

Gruber froze and the crowd fell silent. The girl's cheeks turned red. Gaylord whirled.

Lew Morrell, standing by the hitchrack, picking his teeth, grinned lewdly. "Prime stuff, huh, Sheriff? Be a good boy and shoot some more little ranchers and maybe Gruber'll let you make some time with her."

Gaylord stared at him for a moment, fighting back the red flare of rage. "Morrell," he said, "you'll apologize. To Miss Gruber, to Major Gruber, to me, and to this town. And then you'll get out of Warshield fast and you'd better not come back."

Morrell straightened up and spat into the dust. There was a glint in his eyes that Gaylord recognized; he knew what Morrell wanted, and he sighed. Well, he was in a mood to give it to him. The shooting, then Clint's resignation, Carla's needling him—he'd had enough. He needed

GAYLORD'S BADGE

someone he could get his hands on, an outlet for all the rage and tensions swirling in him. "All right," he said quietly. "Over yonder in the middle of the street."

Morrell did not move. "That where you carry out the executions?" He looked at the Colt on Gaylord's hip.

"No," Gaylord said. "That's where I'm gonna beat the grease outa you."

"Frank," said Gruber, at his elbow. "Chain can handle—"

"He ain't heeled; I want no bloodshed," Gaylord said. "And it's me he's laid his mouth on, too. He's mine. Don't anybody else mess in. I'll have the hide of the man who does." Then his hand went to the buckle of his gunbelt. "Hold this."

Morrell grinned but his eyes were as hard as agates. "You mean that? You and me straight up and no guns, no interference?"

"It's what you been faunchin' for, ain't it?"

"Yeah," Morrell said. "It ain't much, but it's better than nothin' when it comes to makin' you pay for what you did to those two cowboys last night." Then, coolly, he turned away and strode to the middle of the street.

"Mr. Gaylord—" the girl said, voice quavering.

"Hush, Florence," Gruber cut in. Gaylord strode out to face Morrell, who waited, thumbs hooked in belt. This man would be no cinch to take; the match was even—and the way he felt just now, that suited him fine. For the moment he was no longer Frank Gaylord, lawman, but savoring the luxury of being Frank Gaylord, private citizen, with an enemy that he could get his hands on waiting for him.

Now, save for the stamping of the coach horses and the distant braying of a mule, the main street of Warshield

39

MADISON COUNTY.
CANTON PUBLIC LIBRARY SYSTEM
CANTON. MISS. 39046

was still, hushed. The wind rattled the sign over Needham's Store.

"Come and git me, Gaylord," Morrell said, and he spat
again.

"Comin'." Then, knowing that it was unwise, but too
wound up for wisdom, Gaylord charged in.

A mistake, all right, because Morrell was blacksnake-
swift. He pivoted, dropped into a crouch, and the fist
Gaylord aimed at his head missed, and Gaylord's other
hand bounced off his shoulder, and then a mule seemed to
kick Gaylord in the ribs. His breath went out in a whoosh,
and before he could recover, that mule's hoof collided
with his chin, and he was slammed back hard against the
coach's high back wheel. The street seemed to tilt, blur,
and then Morrell was coming, his fist huge in Gaylord's
vision, aimed at Gaylord's nose. Frank jerked aside his
head; knuckles raked his cheek and Morrell grunted and
slammed up hard against him and they grappled. All this
in a pair of seconds; Morrell gave him no time to get his
balance. His hands tangled in Gaylord's hair; he slammed
the sheriff's head against the coach. Gaylord saw flaring
lights; instinctively he pounded Morrell in the flanks, the
kidneys. Morrell's knee came up for his groin, but Gaylord's thigh deflected it. Then, with all of his strength,
Gaylord came off of the wheel, and, locked together, they
staggered to the middle of the street. Both let go simultaneously and began to slug it out, without science, without
footwork, two big men dealing each other terrible punish-
ment and taking it. Gaylord's whole body shook with the
impact of Morrell's fists and with the shock of his own
landing on Morrell's body. Neither had gotten a clean
blow at the face; they were too close. Then Morrell
stepped back to get that slack, and Gaylord would not let

him have it. He was going to end this and end it quickly. He charged in hard, his body collided with Morrell's and rocked it, and he seized both of Morrell's shoulders and ducked his head. Morrell cursed and tried to get up his hands, but Gaylord's head came up, hard, and his skull caught Morrell on the chin and snapped back his head. Morrell sighed, and now Gaylord stepped back. Morrell tried to recover, but a fraction too late; his hands were slow coming up to guard, and Gaylord hit low, in the belly, just below the breastbone. Foul breath and spittle sprayed him as Morrell half doubled over, and Gaylord had a second, then, to aim the next blow. It caught Morrell on his jaw's curve, and split the skin and meat on Gaylord's knuckles. Morrell's head whipped all the way around. His hands dropped and his legs seemed boneless. Gaylord knew, from the shock of the blow traveling up his arm and through his body, that it was over. He stepped back, and Lew Morrell flopped limply into the dust at Gaylord's feet and did not move.

For a moment Gaylord stared down at him. Then the mist of combat ebbed from his brain; he was sober, clear-headed, but panting for breath, aching in every muscle. He dug a handkerchief from his back pocket and applied it to his split cheek. Then, unsteadily, he turned to face the crowd—and stare into the excited blue eyes of Florence Gruber. "Mr. Gaylord," she whispered, and then moved forward as if to try to help him.

"I'll be all right. Look out, you'll git blood all over you."

"He's right, Florence. You'll ruin your dress." Gruber caught her, pulled her back. Then he himself stepped forward. "Frank, that was a damned good piece of work. I'm grateful to you."

Gaylord sucked in wind. "Just sorry Miss Gruber had to see that kind of mess. . . ."

Gruber's mouth twisted. "Well, she might as well get used to Wyoming." He handed the sheriff his gun. "Listen, we've got to go now. But don't forget. Chain, next Saturday night. Be there for sure."

"Yeah," Gaylord said. "I'll be there."

Flanked by his bodyguards, Gruber turned away. His sister cast one more look over her shoulder as he led her down the sidewalk.

"Frank." It was Tom Callaway, now his chief deputy. "Man, you wiped him out. But he plowed you up some."

"I'm okay," Gaylord said, buckling on his gun. He looked at the sprawled form in the dusty street. "But, Lord God, I'm tired." He gestured. "Git him in a cell, will you; disorderly conduct, somethin' like that. Better have Doc Larkins take a look at him."

"I'll see to it," Tom said.

"Good. I'll palaver with him later, when he's able to talk." He turned away, legs unsteady, and started up the street. Instinctively he made for Carla Doane's house, wanting to feel her touch, have her wash and bandage him. But after a few strides he halted. No. Not after this morning. And besides, this fight had been over another woman—or at least she would see it that way.

Gaylord stood there for a moment, then crossed the street and made for Garrison's Hotel.

CHAPTER IV

"Gentlemen." Standing, Ross Gruber raised his long-stemmed glass. "Gentlemen, I give you Wyoming."

Like all the other men present at the long table in the big dining room of the Chain Ranch house, Frank Gaylord rose. "Wyoming." A dozen voices murmured echo to the toast and everyone drank. Then the men sat down again, and a Chinese servant brought in the brandy and the cigars. Chairs scuffed as the men closed up, the ladies having already withdrawn.

"Frank," Gruber said, smiling. "Why don't you come up here and sit by me?"

Gaylord nodded and, a little uncomfortable in boiled shirt and tie and blue suit, took the chair on the Chain manager's right, the one which until a few moments ago had been occupied by Florence Gruber.

There was a moment, then, while the men lit their cigars. Gaylord looked at them through the curling smoke of his own good Havana. A powerful man himself, he responded to power; and this room was full of it. Gathered here were the movers and shakers of Colter County, indeed, of this half of Wyoming. Some, like Gruber, were Americans, hardbitten men who owned or managed for others millions of acres of range and uncounted thousands of head of cattle, mostly well bred-up with Angus and Galloway blood now from the original longhorn stock.

Others were foreigners, overseeing their own invest-
ments: he counted two Englishmen and one Scot in the
group. Yes, he thought, you could almost smell the power
in this room—and the money: a tang like the aftertaste of
powdersmoke.

It was Lord MacAlpine, the Scot, a leathery-faced man
in his fifties, sitting across from Gruber, who spoke first
after the cigars were going. "Your toast amused me, Mr.
Gruber. 'I give you Wyoming.'" He laughed raspingly.
"Nobody gives you anything. You have to take it and hold
on to it."

Beside him, Martin Shell, owner of a huge spread in the
Sweetwater country, chuckled. A short, squarely built
man with a poll of curly black hair, he took his cigar from
his mouth. "Well, we've done that, ain't we?"

"Not yet," MacAlpine snapped. "We lack considerable
of being able to make that claim, Mr. Shell." He looked
up and down the table. "Or maybe your profits haven't
dropped this year as mine have. I say who owns Wyoming
is still an open question. We've made progress, yes. But
relax, close our eyes for only a moment—'a little sleep, a
little slumber,' as the Good Book says—and we'll wake up
to find we've lost it. That the damned rustlers and mavericks have stolen it out from under all our noses."

"Well, they're tryin', and that's a fact," Jim Whitworth
from Carbon County growled. "Between the rustlin' and
the market droppin', I'm gittin' pinched, and pinched
damned bad. With prices comin' down in Chicago the
way they are, not to mention Kansas City, I'm at the point
where I can't afford to lose a single slick-eared calf. I
didn't fight the damned Sioux and Cheyennes to set up
my spread to have a bunch of long-loopin' greasy-sackers
pick me clean!"

"And yet that's what it's coming to!" MacAlpine rasped.
"A fight! Sooner or later we'll have to take some action—and I say sooner!"

Gaylord sipped his brandy as a murmur of assent arose
around the table, and a chill of foreboding walked down
his spine. There was, he thought, something unreal about
all this. These men had thousands, hundreds of thousands
of dollars—some of them, millions—and yet you'd think
that the loss of a single calf would shove them over bank-
ruptcy's edge. For a moment, the brandy tasted bitter. He
thought of Phil Hoff, Billy Dann—and saw Clint Wallace
flinging down his badge again. Maybe he was out of place
here, maybe . . . and maybe not. Maybe this was the way
you had to be to get anywhere in life—and God knows he
was tired of being bellied down like a wagon in the mud.
If he ever was to get unstuck, amount to anything in Wyoming, he'd better change his thinking—start thinking the
way they did, not like some penny-ante nester, thirty-a-
month cowboy. After all, he had to get reelected this year,
and without the support of Gruber and men like him
there was no chance. He drank another swallow; this one
went down easier. Then, as he set down the glass, he saw
it on the table—a single yellow hair, long, silky, golden
against the white of the cloth.

And now, although Gruber was talking, Gaylord was
not listening. He was thinking of Florence. And feeling
something stir within him that he hesitated to put a name
to.

When he had arrived at Chain a lot of guests were already present, but she had singled him out among them.
And she was something to take away any man's breath, in
her white dress trimmed with gold, leaving her shoulders
bare, and baring, too, the rounding intimations of her

breasts. Her voice was soft, slightly husky; and one gloved
hand had rested on his wrist. "Sheriff Gaylord. How nice
to see you." Then she was all concern. "That cut on your
cheek. I hope it's healing well."

"Don't even know it's there."

"Well, I should think you would." The blue eyes met
his directly, and she laughed a little. "What an introduc-
tion to your territory! Ross had written me about the remarkable qualities of Wyoming men, but still, such gal-
lantry . . . one hardly finds it in the East anymore. I'm
afraid chivalry's quite dead in Philadelphia. Of course, I
detest violence . . . and yet, I must confess, it's pretty ex-
citing to have someone you don't even know defend your
honor the way you did mine." Her fingers tightened on his
wrist. "Ross and I both are in your debt."

"Not at all, Miss Gruber. The man was creating a public
disturbance. And . . . maybe I didn't handle it as I should
have. Maybe I should have just run him in. But I was . . .
kind of on edge."

"I should think so, after a brush with death with a couple of outlaws the night before."

"They weren't—"

But he had no chance to finish, as she went on: "Anyhow, Sheriff, I think you'll always be rather special to me
among the men I may get to know out here. I hope you
don't mind, but I've asked Ross to seat us together at
dinner."

"No, I don't mind. It pleases me."

"Good. After what you did for us, I think pleasing you
is my obligation. Now, if you'll excuse me . . ." Then she
was gone, to greet someone else. But, circulating in the
crowd, Gaylord was acutely aware of the place on his
wrist where her hand had rested, and even in the smoke

and smell of whiskey her perfume seemed to linger in his nostrils.

He had been pleased to see that everyone here seemed to know him, either by sight or reputation. In fact, Mac-Alpine had put it into words: "Yes, of course, Frank Gaylord. Ross Gruber tells me you're a coming man in this part of Wyoming."

Heady stuff, as heady as the champagne and wine at dinner, and the undivided attention of Florence Gruber beside him, between Gaylord and her brother. And it was curious: only once tonight had he thought of Carla Doane, and then only to realize that she was easily ten years older than Florence Gruber. . . .

Carefully he picked up the single strand of hair, drew its silken length across a calloused finger. Then, slowly, he came back to the present, as Gruber's words impinged on his consciousness.

"Well, part of the reason I asked everyone here tonight is to get these matters hammered out. We've got a lot of problems we've got to deal with, and when I report to my principles in England I'd like to be able to say we've made progress, taken definite action."

Taking his cigar from his mouth, Gruber went on: "We've got our usual problem of losses. With prices down and costs up, every calf we lose means that much less profit. That's why I say we've got to crack down harder on these people coming in here, preempting our range and water, and using long ropes and running irons to put themselves in business. As far as I'm concerned, every little nonassociation rancher's nothing but a rustler, when you come down to it, and the time is past for dilly-dallying. We're going to have to start cleaning them out before they nibble us to death!"

"Absolutely!" MacAlpine struck the table with his hand.

"And another thing's the cowboys," Gruber said. "They're just as bad. They work for us from spring until fall roundup, and then, apparently, think they're entitled to live off us through the winter. All right, we've closed down the grubline, so they can't hang around the way they used to. With any luck, when winter comes, that'll keep 'em moving on to Montana or Dakota or somewhere else where the ranchers haven't got sense enough not to make suckers out of themselves. Anyhow, there's no doubt about it, this winter we've got to be even harder about havin' idle, unemployed riders hanging around. Because when they've got no work, they'll support themselves by stealing. A cowboy not on a payroll is a thief, as far as I'm concerned, and there's no place for him in Colter County until he's needed in the spring again."

Martin Shell, from the Sweetwater, spoke up. "That's pretty rough talk, Ross."

"Rough?" Gruber looked at him. "It's common sense."

"Maybe the way you look at it back East—or across the ocean, Lord MacAlpine. But we've never treated honest waddies like that out here before. Closin' down the grub-line's bad enough. That's like slappin' a man in the face. Roustin' him because he's got no work when there's none to be had is worse." He looked up and down the table. "You want to be careful you don't push 'em too hard. These ain't factory hands or peasants or whatever you call 'em. These are men who'll fight back if you put 'em between a rock and a hard place."

Sir Randolph Hart, one of the English ranchers at the table, stood up, tall and dapper. "Then let them fight. The sooner they are put in their place and learn to stay there, the better! I, for one, am tired of the arrogance and disrespect of your lower classes out here! They need a lesson, and a damned good one!"

Shell snorted. "It might be somebody else who'll get a lesson, you talk like that. If they pull off this strike they're talking about come next spring, you'll see what I mean."

Gruber said, "There'll be no strike. I promise you that."

"A big promise," Shell said, unawed.

"I can't speak for the Sweetwater," Gruber went on, "but there'll be none in Colter County. And I think the man on my right is ample guarantee of that."

He smiled, then went on crisply: "Sheriff Frank Gaylord's the kind of lawman each of you should have in your own county. Let me tell you what he's done in just the past week. Two of the most troublesome agitators among the cowboys in this county were a pair of little ranchers—rustlers, really—named Dann and Hoff. I swore out warrants against them for cattle theft. Gaylord served them the way they should be served. Hoff tried to resist and got short shrift; he's dead. Dann's in jail, awaiting trial. And, if that weren't enough, Gaylord also dealt a first-class beating to a drifter who, in all probability, is an organizer for the Knights of Labor. He worked him over good and threw him in a cell, where I trust he'll be in cold storage for a long time. Right, Frank?"

Gaylord said, "I'm afraid not. I had to release him next day."

"You what?" Gruber frowned.

"The most I could charge him with was disorderly conduct. He paid the fine, so I had to let him go. But I warned him to get out of the county and not come back. If he did, I told him, I'd haul him in again as a vagrant."

"That's too bad," Gruber said. "Still . . . if you've made

him leave the county, I suppose that will have to serve. All the same, you've set an example this week for everyone to follow."

He faced the men at the table. "Anyway, that's how we handle the threat of a strike—or anything else against the association's interest—here in Colter County. And, I'm proud to say, the sheriff plans to stand for reelection, and Chain will see that he remains in office." He paused. "There you have it, gentlemen. My suggestion is that each and every one of us bear down and bear down hard. Keep the grubline closed. Harass the rustling little ranchers without mercy. Don't yield one inch to the preposterous demands of the cowboys. If you have trouble with a rider, circulate his name, and we'll make sure he'll never work for an association ranch again. We've got to be hard if we're to survive this slump! Damned hard!"

"There's a difference between bein' hard and bein' a damned fool," Martin Shell rasped.

Gruber turned on him. "Martin, sometimes I wonder if you're with us or against us."

"I'm with you," Shell said. "I'm a member of the association and I've got no choice. But I'll speak my mind. And—" His eyes shuttled to Gaylord. "And I'd like to hear the sheriff speak his. Gaylord, I've heard of you and have always admired the rep you have. What's your opinion, since you're the one responsible for keepin' order here? You agree with Ross? The thing to do is throw a man in jail or shoot him or blacklist him or starve him the minute he gets crosswise of the association? Or do you agree with me—that, by damn, these tactics will backfire sooner or later? What's your thoughts?"

Gaylord hesitated, aware of all eyes on him. In his own mind he was clear: Shell was right, absolutely right. But if he wanted to be reelected, to admit that now would be to lose Gruber's confidence, maybe turn Chain Ranch against him. And without Chain's backing he would be through here.

His mouth thinned: this was not a choice he'd ever had to make before; at no time had he, in his whole life, ever hesitated to say exactly what he thought. And, by damn, he told himself, he was too old to start pussyfooting now. Slowly he got to his feet.

But before he could speak a door across the room opened and Florence Gruber stood there, come, probably, to tell the men they'd lingered too long, to come join the ladies. Gaylord was looking straight at her, and she met his eyes and smiled.

And suddenly Gaylord could not do it. Because Gruber controlled everything Frank Gaylord valued—his badge, his future prosperity . . . and this woman.

Because he wanted her; he knew that, in this moment. He desired her in a way and with an urgency that he had never wanted any other woman. And suddenly he knew, with a flash of insight, that she was not beyond his reach. Not if he played his cards right, not if he stuck with Chain.

"I think there's some points to think about in what Mr. Shell has said," he heard himself begin. "But maybe . . . maybe you have to use different ways in different sections. All I know is that I don't make the laws. That's done by the legislature in Cheyenne, the county board here in Colter. And whatever the legislature and the board say is the law is what I enforce. I try to do it without fear or favor. That's what I get paid for and all I get paid for." He hesitated, the things he should have been saying backing up in his throat, refusing to come out. "The law protects every man's rights," he ended. "If it don't, it should be changed." And he sat down.

He saw Shell looking at him with a mixture of amusement and contempt that made him feel smaller, dirty. But Florence's eyes still held him, and her smile now was for himself alone.

There was, then, for half a minute, silence. Finally Gruber smiled. "I think Sheriff Gaylord's put it in a nutshell. The laws protect our rights. All we need is men of Frank Gaylord's caliber to enforce 'em. Now, gentlemen, shall we join the ladies?"

After that, for Gaylord, the evening was a blur, dominated by her presence. Attaching herself to him, she was by him constantly, laughing at his jokes, asking questions about the West and his life and work, listening to the answers intently. Blue eyes, blond hair, the scent of perfume, light gleaming on those ivory shoulders . . . It had been a long time since Gaylord had felt so young, witty, carefree, a long time since he had laughed so readily. Only once he thought of Carla—but then only to compare her with Florence Gruber. There was no comparison, and, feeling a little shamed, he quickly put Carla from his mind.

Meanwhile, he was alert to all around him. Here was Wyoming behind the scenes, the men who made the wheels turn. American and foreign, they had one thing in common—a hard, practical respect only for the dollar . . . unless you excepted Martin Shell. The man from the Sweetwater sidled up to Gaylord in the parlor. "Sheriff, I had hoped you'd back me up. There are a lot of things need saying to this crowd."

"Sorry if I disappointed you, Mr. Shell. But I run my office and I let you folks run your ranches."

"Sho. I reckon that's how a man gets along." Shell turned and ambled off, reminding Gaylord of a solitary old bull buffalo on the outskirts of a herd.

Then Gruber nudged his elbow. "Frank. See you alone a minute? Florence, you'll excuse us?"

"Of course. But don't keep Mr. Gaylord from me long."

They went into Gruber's office and the major shut the door. "Drink?" He poured shots from a bourbon bottle, handed Gaylord a glass, and stood there facing him, a stocky, impressive man. "Cheers." They drank.

Then Gruber said, "Frank, you had me worried for just a minute there at dinner, but you pulled out of it very nicely. All in all, you've made a good impression to-night—a damned good one." Then he smiled. "Especially on my sister."

Gaylord acknowledged that with a nod.

"Anyhow," Gruber continued, "you heard what *I* said when I introduced you. I intend to see you reelected. And, in due time, I'd like to see you in a higher office than just a county sheriff's. We need men like you in Cheyenne . . . but that's something for the future. Anyhow, I guarantee you this, stick with Chain—and with the association—and you'll do well. We've got plans for you." He smiled. "I wouldn't be surprised if my sister has, too, but that's her affair—and yours."

Gaylord stiffened and his pulse beat quicker. It was a moment before his attention came back to Gruber.

"But I was serious tonight about this rustling problem," Gruber was saying. "You've struck some good licks lately, yeah; but you got to strike some more, and fast. There's still a lot of troublemakers running loose. You know and I know that they're wide-looping. And I'll be blunt—it's up to you to start taking them out of circulation . . . and fast. Men like Chris Dennison and that fellow over in Horn's Coulee, Parker's his name. And . . . hell, you know the ones I mean as well as I do. Hoff and Dann were just a start. I hope you'll be moving soon against these other rustlers."

Gaylord stared at him. "Now, wait, Major—"

"I can't wait!" Gruber snapped. "The members of the English syndicate that own Chain—my bosses—are unhappy as hell with my profit figures. There's talk of some of them coming here on an inspection tour. Maybe even a surprise arrival, with no warning. Well, if that happens I want to be ready for it. I want to show them that positive action's being taken. And that means putting a lot of people in the penitentiary!"

Gaylord drew in breath. "If you want to swear out warrants, I'll serve 'em. But you'll have to have a case, some evidence." His voice was cold; he was out of the clouds now and not liking the drift of this conversation.

Gruber sensed that, and his eyes shifted. "I'm not ready to swear out warrants. And as for building the cases, getting the evidence, that's the sheriff's job—isn't it?" Before Gaylord could answer, he went on: "I think that's the most important thing you've got to do. That, and make sure every agitator for a cowboy strike gets what's coming to him. It's too damned bad you had to let Morrell go. That doesn't please me."

"I had no choice," Gaylord said.

"Well, next time arrange things so you have, if you see what I mean."

Gaylord opened his mouth, then closed it again. "Anyhow," Gruber said, "the main thing is, you've chased him out of Colter County." Then he smiled and touched Gaylord on the arm. "I'm not criticizing the way you run your office. Just offering suggestions. Now, run on. Florence will be hacked at me anyhow for keeping you tied up this long."

CHAPTER V

Sunrise spilled brightness across the enormous land as Gaylord rode at a high lope toward Warshield. The hooves of his big sorrel drummed with a steady rhythm; the wind was fresh and clean and cool in his face, sweet with sage. Larks whirled and called, once a band of antelope rocked away toward the horizon, white flags bouncing. It was the kind of morning to match Frank Gaylord's mood.

Last night it seemed like a whole new world had opened up for him. Not just the promise of money and power, implicit in his acceptance by Gruber and the others as one of them, a man of consequence: it was Florence who made all the difference, Florence who'd changed everything.

Some of the guests had gone, others were inside with Gruber, when he and she, at her suggestion, strolled out on the porch. Overhead, the sky was powdered white with stars; in the distance, a wolf howled like a lost soul just comprehending the eternity of its doom. Florence leaned against him. "What a country," she whispered. "What a marvelous, magnificent country."

Her head was close to his; he smelled the perfume in her hair. "Wyoming's a fine place," he said.

"I'm coming to love it," she answered. "I may stay a

long, long time." She flung out an arm. "Who knows, I may stay forever!"

"Ross would like that," Gaylord said.

She turned her head and looked up at him, eyes vivid in the starlight. "Only Ross?"

What happened next was smooth, natural, and instinctive. She had wanted him to kiss her, and Gaylord did. Her lips were soft, her body warm and curved as she pressed against him for a moment. And then, easily, she pulled away, looking up at him, and now her eyes were grave and serious.

"Only Ross?" she whispered again.

"No," Gaylord said. "Not just Ross."

He reached for her once more, but this time she eluded him. "No, Frank. Perhaps we'd better not."

Gaylord did not answer.

She looked away. "As it is, you'll think I'm forward, maybe worse than that."

Gaylord said, "No. No, I don't think you're forward. I think—" He broke off, afraid to say it, having no right to.

She said, in a voice of curious quietness, "Maybe neither one of us should say what he thinks. Not just now. After all, we've hardly met. And yet . . . No. No, let's not talk any more. Let's go inside. People will be wondering where we are."

"Yes," Gaylord said. She took his arm and they went back into the house. But already the world had changed. He knew it and he knew she knew it, too.

He had seen that knowledge in her eyes when, well after midnight, he had said his goodbyes to Gruber and those guests staying overnight. "Frank," she'd whispered, when the two of them were for a moment by themselves. "You'll come back often?"

"Every chance I get."

"Good. And as often as I can, I'll come to town." She smiled, holding his hands. "Good night, Frank."

She vanished into the corridor. Gruber strolled with Gaylord to the porch, where one of the Chain men had the sorrel waiting. "Wish you'd stay the night, Frank."

"Like to, but I've got to relieve Tom Callaway. And it's a middling ride to Warshield."

"All right." Then Gruber was serious. "But remember our little talk in my office. Bear down on these rustlers, will you? And I mean hard."

"Yes," Gaylord said. "I'll do that. Enjoyed it, Major. Good night." He stepped into the stirrup, swung up, and touched the sorrel with spurs. It trotted out of the Chain Ranch yard, its rider impatient to be alone with the new thoughts and dreams crowding in his head.

And now, he thought, riding through the dawn, he had it all straight, all worked out. He would settle for no less than Florence Gruber and money enough to support her in her kind of style. And that meant holding the confidence of her brother, of the other big ranchers, of the association. It meant taking what they offered and giving fair value in return. Carla, of course, would say that he had been corrupted—but what did Carla know? He was entitled to what he could get. Besides, if he, Frank Gaylord, wasn't reelected, Chain would certainly put somebody in his place whom Gruber could control completely. The cowboys and little ranchers would be even worse off then. No, he owed it to them as much as to the association to make sure he stayed on as sheriff here. After all, when he had a new four-year term he'd be secure, have a base to work from to straighten out all this trouble, get all parties in Colter County satisfied, and put an end to all this strife. And still stride out toward the new goals he'd glimpsed tonight.

Grinning, he reached inside his coat for a cigar; and a paper rustled in his pocket. Then he remembered: the bill of sale he'd written out for fifty head of cattle—Clint Wallace's wedding present. There'd been no opportunity to give it to the couple at the brief wedding ceremony before the judge; and later, when he'd gone down to the little house in the creekbottom where Joey, Clint's new wife, had been living, they were gone.

Now Gaylord's grin broadened. Well, from where he was right now, a half hour would see him at the spring on the homestead where Clint would build his house. And suddenly he wanted very much to see Wallace again, have breakfast with the newlyweds, and watch Clint's response to his gift. The cattle, of course, were really from Gruber, but except for Frank Gaylord, Gruber would not have given them, so they were really from him, too. He turned the sorrel and loped it off the road.

———————————

The range Wallace had taken up was a fine scope of land, with ample water and good grass. A ridge above a year-round spring provided shelter for the house and layout he would build. But for the time being there was only a sheepherder's wagon parked there, which would serve the couple as a home until Clint could erect a more permanent dwelling. Nearing it, Gaylord reined in. They were there, all right; a curl of smoke rose from a campfire. He put the sorrel into a walk. "Hello, the wagon!" he called as he approached.

From behind it a small, trim figure clad in shirt and

Levis appeared, a rifle in its hands. Gaylord grinned. "Ease off, Joey! It's me, Frank Gaylord! Come to say hello!"

Joey Wallace halted, staring at him. Gaylord advanced. He had often enough seen her strut her stuff in scanty clothes in the dance hall where she'd worked; now, not even the faded man's garb she wore could disguise her perky beauty, her dancer's grace. Her hair was sand-colored, her eyes big and gray, her nose short and tilted. Her face, just now, was smudged with campfire ash.

Recognizing Gaylord, she lowered the Winchester car-bine, and he saw her shoulders slump with relief. "Good morning, Sheriff." Her voice was cool, neither welcoming nor hostile.

Gaylord swung down and groundhitched the sorrel. "Well," he said jovially, "where's your old man, Miz Wal-lace? Was hoping maybe you could rustle up a cup of coffee for me, maybe even some breakfast. Got some news for you and Clint I think you'll like."

"The coffee's hot," she said, "and I'll be glad to fix you breakfast. But I'm afraid Clint's not here. He pulled out before light, headed for town."

"Oh. Well, I reckon I'll see him there. Still, I'd appreci-ate the coffee if you could spare it." Gaylord shrugged off his disappointment.

"Plenty made, and it's hot." For the first time she smiled. It was remarkable, Gaylord thought. She was what—about twenty-one, twenty-two; and, maybe since the age of sixteen, she had made her living in a hard, maybe even ugly, way. Yet that part of her life seemed to have left no mark, and, if anything, she was prettier and more appealing in her denim with her smudged face than she had been in her floozy dress with paint on her lips and cheeks.

As she poured coffee from a big enamel pot on the coals, Gaylord looked around. There had been some digging in the ridge's base, the earth laid bare. Otherwise, save for the wagon, so far there was nothing. They had a long, hard row to hoe ahead of them, the Wallaces—and yet Gaylord could not suppress a kind of surge of envy of Clint. He had really found himself a woman.

But then it passed. So have I, Gaylord thought. And I won't have to ask her to live in no sheepherder's wagon, either. He took the coffee. "Obliged, Miz Wallace."

She smiled. "Joey."

"Joey." He sipped the scalding brew, relieved. So they could still be friends. It was hell when their women turned their men against their old *compañeros*. "So Clint's gone to Warshield, eh? What for?"

"Just business." The gray eyes flickered away.

He nodded. "Looks like you're making progress here."

"Some. We'll build a soddy to start with. Then some corrals. Can't afford much store-bought stuff. Don't have much money, and what we've got has to go into stock." She poured coffee for herself. "Clint and I agreed—we can live hard for a while. Main thing's to build for the future."

"Right. Everybody's got to think about the future." Gaylord leaned back against the wagon wheel, fished in his pocket. "Take a look at this, Joey. I hope it will help the future a little bit." He handed her the bill of sale.

Joey took it almost suspiciously, opened it, and read it. Her eyes widened and she let out a breath of awe. "Fifty head . . ." Then, unexpectedly, her mouth thinned. She passed it back. "I guess you'd better give it to Clint and let him decide whether we'll take it or not."

Gaylord rose. "What?"

Her face was flushed; she bit her lip. "He said we had to look out for presents from you. They might be bribes from Gruber."

"Now, wait," Gaylord said.

"I'm sorry, Sheriff. I'm just telling you how Clint feels. He . . . he thinks a lot of you, but he says we've got to face it: to make it here we'll have to buck Chain. And you're on Chain's side, and . . ."

"I'm not on anybody's side," Gaylord said harshly. "And damn it, girl, Clint ought to know that."

Joey looked away. "Just talk it out with him in Warshield. It's not my business, it's his. I—" She broke off, and Gaylord turned, because hoofbeats, a horse coming fast, then slowing, drummed beneath her words. A voice, vaguely familiar to Gaylord, called out, "Hello, the wagon! Joey—?"

"Easy," Frank Gaylord said. Hand on his Colt, he stepped over the wagon tongue.

The rider on the dun horse sat up straight, face twisted in surprise at the sight of Gaylord. Then the man recovered, and a slow grin lifted his lips, showing stained teeth. "Hello, Gaylord," he said.

"Morrell," Gaylord said.

"That's right." Lew Morrell, face still showing the marks of his fight with Gaylord, raised both hands high. "I'm still not heeled, Sheriff." Then he swung down, dropping his mount's reins.

Gaylord said, "You're supposed to stay out of Colter County. You were rousted."

"Because I had no job. A vagrant. Well, I got a job, now. I'm an employee of a Colter County rancher, and that means I got a right to be here."

"A Colter County rancher—"

Morrell's mocking smile widened. "Billy Dann," he said. "He took me on to look after his place if he went to prison. Or to help him if he makes bail." He took a step forward. "So, can you still roust me, Sheriff?"

Gaylord sucked in breath. "I can do any goddamned thing I take a notion to in Colter County," he said harshly.

"I mean legally," Morrell said.

Before Gaylord could answer, Joey Wallace was at his side. "Hello, Lew."

"Joey."

Gaylord looked at her in surprise. "You two know each other?"

"He's a friend of Clint's. He's helping us get settled in. He's here today to work on the soddy while Clint's in town."

Gaylord said, "Maybe he's a friend of Clint's and maybe not. Me, I'd say he's not a man you'd do well to get mixed up with. You heard what happened in Warshield—"

"We heard," said Joey.

After a moment Gaylord said, "All right. Clint's a grown man." He kept his voice even, not betraying the irritation and even the sadness he felt at this sign of the widening gulf between himself and Wallace. He turned to Morrell. "All right, I am not going to roust you. But I am sure as hell going to keep an eye on you. If you even spit on the street while you're in Warshield, you're in bad trouble. Bear that in mind."

Morrell only grinned faintly, his eyes still chill.

"Anyhow, thanks for the coffee, Joey." Gaylord mounted, turned the horse. Once he looked over his shoulder as he rode away. Morrell was watching him, and Joey was pouring another cup of coffee for the man.

———————————

"Bail?" Gaylord said incredulously, three hours later.

"Bail," Tom Callaway answered. The chief deputy was tall, lanky, with a cowhorn mustache draping a pinched mouth. "They come down here jest after breakfast, Clint Wallace and that lawyer, Terry Fielding. They had a note from Judge Merkel sayin' to send Billy Dann up to the courthouse for a hearin' on makin' bond. I sent him up there in cuffs, with Jonas to guard him. They come back a little while ago with an order for his release. Seems that, under the law, there was nothing the judge could do but grant it, Jonas said. But Merkel set it so high, he figured Billy didn't have a chance of payin' it, three thousand dollars. But he didn't count on Carla Doane. She was with 'em and she laid it out then and there—in cash."

"Carla?" Gaylord stared at him.

"Right. So, there was nothin' I could do but turn Dann loose. He's free as an antelope right now. He and Clint and Fielding all went off together. And . . . oh, yeah. Carla sent this to you by Jonas." He handed Frank Gaylord a sealed envelope.

Gaylord, trying to make sense of all this, ripped it open. The note inside said:

Frank, I know this morning's events will disturb you. Please, as soon as you're back in town, come to see me and I'll try to explain. Love, C.

Gaylord rammed the note in his pocket. *I'll see you, all right*, he thought grimly. "Anybody wants me," he told Callaway, "I'll be at Mrs. Doane's." And he whirled, went out of the office.

Taking a sidestreet, he tried to make sense out of all this. Clint and Dann and Morrell and Fielding . . . The latter was a lean, gray-faced young man who'd come to Warshield six months ago, hung out his attorney's shingle, and been a thorn in Gaylord's side ever since. Fielding knew every rule, regulation, and law, federal or territorial, that applied in Wyoming, and he could argue rings around old Judge Merkel or Fred Dall, the county prosecutor, who was also Chain's attorney. It was not often that Fielding, who drank a lot and eked out his income playing poker, got a case; but when he did he usually won. It had been he who'd multiplied Gaylord's paperwork threefold, forcing him to have properly drawn warrants before every arrest, accountings in writing for prisoners' property, a host of other documents with every *i* dotted and every *t* crossed. Still, Gaylord had to admire Fielding: he was honest and he had brass-bound guts. And maybe in the long run Fielding's influence had been beneficial: the pressure he had put on Gaylord had helped build the sheriff's reputation as a stickler for the law. With Fielding around, he dared not be anything else.

Still, this was going to be one hell of a thing to explain to Ross Gruber. And coming on top of Morrell's return. And Clint, he thought with foreboding, mixed in with all of them; and now Carla. Something was brewing here, something he did not like.

At Carla's house he paused for a moment. Then he opened the gate in the picket fence and, instead of circling to the back door, as usual, went up on the front porch and twisted the bell knob. This was official business, and she might as well understand that.

Then he heard footsteps inside; she opened the door, and for an instant it was like old times. The sight of her made his mouth go dry, and for just a moment there was the impulse to reach out and touch her. Then he said tersely: "You sent me a note."

"Yes. Come in, Frank."

He entered the pleasant hall, then halted. There were three hats hanging on the tree there. Carla followed his gaze. "They're back in the kitchen. Come on."

"Who?"

"You'll see." She led him through the house. At the kitchen door she stood aside. "Go ahead."

Gaylord entered, and then stopped short.

"Hello, Frank," Clint Wallace said. With Billy Dann and the lawyer, Terence Fielding, he sat at the kitchen table, drinking coffee.

Gaylord's eyes ranged over them, then went to Carla. "What the hell is this?" he asked softly.

Clint rose, smiling. "Ease off, Frank. We're all your friends. Even Billy. He don't hold it against you for doing your duty." He came forward and put out his hand.

Gaylord took it, and Clint's grasp was firm, wholehearted. Gaylord could see the affection in his eyes, and something unknotted within the sheriff. Then Fielding stepped forward.

"Clint's right," he said, smiling. "We all are your well-wishers, Sheriff Gaylord, even if we've had to oppose you, so to speak, this morning. And all we want is a few minutes of your time while we talk a little politics."

"Politics?" Gaylord blinked.

"That's right." Clint grinned. "We want you to run for sheriff again."

Gaylord shook his head uncomprehendingly. "I aim to."

"Yes," Fielding said crisply. "But under Gruber's sponsorship, on the association ticket. But we've got something else in mind. What we're going to ask you to do is break with Chain, and not run for it, but against it."

CHAPTER VI

Gaylord, not quite believing what he had heard, looked at them, and Clint laughed softly.

"You think we're crazy, huh, Frank? Well, maybe we are and maybe we ain't. Anyhow— Carla, why don't you pour him a cup of coffee while Terry explains."

Gaylord nodded grimly. If Clint was driving at what he seemed to be . . . He pulled out a chair. "Yeah, Fielding. Say your piece."

The lawyer was really not much older than Clint Wallace, an intense grayhound of a man in clean, but shabby town clothes. His dark eyes flashed with intensity and conviction as he began.

"Well, it's something I've had in my mind since not long after I came to Colter County. The fact of the matter is, when I saw how things stacked up here I was shocked." His mouth twisted wryly. "You see, I've got an unfortunate failing, Sheriff. I believe in the law, and in every man's equality before it. But here in Wyoming there is no equality before the law—because the laws have been made to be unequal, to give the association men every break and to make it impossible for little ranchers to compete with 'em or cowboys to earn an honest wage. And I can't help it—that kind of thing sticks in my craw. Me, I believe it's time somebody moved to put an end to it, and I don't know of any better place to start than Colter County."

He paused. "So I've been talking to some people. Like Mrs. Doane, here; Clint, Billy Dann, and Phil Hoff before he got shot. And others. Including merchants here in town. And you'd be surprised, Sheriff, at how many folks there are that have a bellyful of being pushed around by Gruber and his kind. They haven't resisted so far, because one man alone or even two can't buck Chain and the association. But in union there is strength. And that's where I come in. Me, and Clint, and Mrs. Doane—and Billy Dann, if he doesn't go to prison first."

Carla set a cup of coffee at Gaylord's elbow, but the sheriff ignored it. "Fielding—"

"Let me finish, please." Spraddle-legged, thumbs hooked in his vest, Fielding faced him. "There are only two ways to fight an outfit like the association. One is with guns. The other is with politics. Well, I'm a man of the law—so guns are out. But politics is a horse of another color." He broke off, gestured. "You're looking at the officers of the Colter County Ranchers and Cowboys Political Committee."

"The what?"

"You heard me." Now Fielding's voice was hard, businesslike. "We're organizing. The little ranchers, any cowboys from the big spreads who have the guts to join us, certain townspeople, everybody who's fed up with Chain. And you might as well get it through your head—politically, we're gonna take over Colter County. And Chain, or anyone else, isn't gonna stop us."

Gaylord digested this for a moment. But he knew politics as well as Fielding did, and— He shook his head. "You're talking through your hat."

"No, I'm not," Fielding rapped. "I know exactly what I'm saying and exactly what I'm doing. I'm not a fool, Sheriff, and I'm not a suckling babe. I'm a politician, and I figure the odds and go with 'em. Well, I've got 'em figured now, and I'm going, and we want you to go, too."

He took a step forward. "I'm not going to tell you in detail what we plan. But I'll say this: Come election time, we'll have a candidate for sheriff on the ballot. We want that candidate to be you. Which means we're asking you to repudiate Chain and the association and put your campaign for reelection in our hands. Then, if you win—and I guarantee that you will—you'll be free of all obligations to Chain Ranch. You can administer the law without fear or favor. That's all we'll ask of you—not one speck more."

Now Gaylord, giving himself time to digest this, sipped the coffee. When he put down the cup he said, "Whose idea was this?"

"The committee was Fielding's idea," Clint Wallace said. "Getting you to run on our ticket was mine. At first Fielding objected. But Carla and I made him see it. That this county couldn't have a better sheriff than you. That right now your hands are tied, but if we could get you loose from Chain you'd be just the man we need." He struck one thigh with his balled fist. "Frank, you got to go with us! We got to have you! Believe me, we're not tryin' to run a sandy. All we're after is to make Colter County a place where people like me and Joey and Billy and all the others can make a decent livin' without worryin' about men bargin' in with guns at night"—his face shadowed—"on trumped-up warrants. Without bein' made outlaws for brandin' their own cattle. Without bein' called rustlers just because we dare to try to raise stock of our own. What about it, Frank? If it meant you could run the law in a county like that, would you tell Chain to go to hell and throw in with us?"

Carla put her hand on his shoulder. "We want you, Frank. We believe in you and we want you to join us."

Gaylord let out a long breath.

"We'd be workin' together again, Frank," Clint said in a low voice. "I'd even come back as chief deputy if you wanted me."

"Even me," Dann said. "Despite what happened the other night, I'm willin' to take my chances in a county where Gaylord runs the law—so long as Gaylord's clear of Chain."

Slowly Frank Gaylord rose, went to the window, and looked out. Somehow, he was not surprised. Sooner or later, it had been bound to come—organized opposition to the association's stranglehold on county politics. For a moment the desire to say yes, to work with Clint, to be free of all obligation to Ross Gruber, was intense. But that was a fuzzy-headed dream. He had to face reality. Besides . . . there was Florence. He seemed to feel again the pressure of her lips, her body pressed close to his.

He played for time. "The kind of thing you're planning costs money," he said. "Where the hell would your kind of people get that kind of money?"

After a moment Carla said, "From me."

Gaylord turned. She was staring at him, face pale, body tense. "Why, it'll clean you out," he said.

"That's a chance I'll have to take. Maybe it will be worth it to me."

He understood, and something stirred within him. To quench it he broke his gaze at her and faced the lawyer.

"You got any idea what you're up against?"

"Plenty," Fielding grinned wryly. "I know all about

Wyoming politics. They—and the elections—are just like everything else out here, wild and woolly and devil-take-the-hindmost."

Then he was serious. "All right. First there are Democratic and Republican precinct conventions. Then the delegates from those nominated county officers at their county conventions. That part of it's normal. The rest is pure Wyoming.

"First of all, there's no registration of voters, no secret ballot, no anything. Anybody who shows up at a polling place can vote, whether he's a drifter passing through, soldiers stationed at a post, underage or overage, or, for that matter, dead or alive. And I know, too, that each big ranch is a polling place—Chain, for instance—and there's nothing in the world to keep Ross Gruber from stuffing a ballot box until it splits its seams."

He paused. "Which leads to another of your weird customs. Once the Democratic and Republican tickets are set, anybody can make up a ballot of his own. He can mix Democrats and Republicans on it, shuffle it around however he pleases. This jolly little arrangement allows anybody who figures he can deliver votes to sell 'em and to collect so much for each ballot for every one of his own slips that ends up in a ballot box. It also tells the candidate hard and clear where his support came from. That's why the association always has a ballot of its own, and why more of those are cast than those cast by Democrats and Republicans put together. To make sure everybody knows who runs the county."

Going to the stove, he refilled his coffee cup. "Now, the shrewd way to handle things would be this: You're a cinch to get on both Democratic and Republican ballots unopposed, with Chain's backing. Once you're on either or both, you'd repudiate Chain publicly. Our committee would handle your campaign and elect you with ballots of its own." He turned. "Like I said, that would be the shrewd way. But we don't want you to be underhanded or beholden to Chain in any way. So what we propose is that you repudiate Chain's support right now. And leave it to us to see that you're nominated by at least one party. That way you'd be clear of Chain right down the line. Sure, Gruber would immediately back an opposition candidate; you wouldn't be a shoo-in. But I still maintain that if you go along with us we'd get you elected."

Gaylord stared at him. "You've lost your mind. That means your committee would have to take over one of the county conventions. You'd have to rip it away from Chain, and Gruber'd never stand for that. You wouldn't have a prayer."

"In our judgment, we'd have more than a prayer." His face was serious. "And get one thing straight, Gaylord. If we elected you, you'd be your own man—all the way down the line."

"I'm my own man now," Gaylord answered sharply. "I always will be."

No one in the room spoke.

Gaylord felt blood mounting to his face. "No. No, I won't go along with this. I'm sorry. But it makes no sense. It would do no good. Nothing would happen except that I'd get whipped and then you'd have a sheriff who really would be Gruber's dog—somebody like that gunman Lang. You get a man like that behind the badge here, you'll really bring down hell on everybody. It's out of the question, Fielding. Things ride as they're set up. If your committee wants to back me, I'll welcome their support, just like I welcome everybody's. And I'll run the law the way I've always done. But as for this scheme of yours . . . count me out."

Again, silence in the room. Then Clint Wallace sighed and stood up. "That's final, Frank?"

"Absolutely."

Clint's lean young face was grim. "All right. We've got another candidate, one well known in the county and a trained law officer. He'll be running against you, then—and I mean hard. And he'll whip you, too, right down into the ground."

"Is that a fact? And who the hell is this?" Gaylord bridled at his tone.

"Me," said Clint.

———————

First there was surprise, then sadness, then fear—and not for himself. "Clint," he said. "You don't want to do that."

"Why not?"

"Because . . . because, damn it, it would only mess you up, at a time when you've just got things going for you. I was out there by your place this morning, and you and Joey are making progress. You'll have a ranch going soon and—" He remembered something then. "The reason I stopped by was to deliver this. A wedding present I never had a chance to give you." He took the bill of sale from his pocket and passed it to Wallace.

Clint unfolded it and read it. For a moment he was silent, but Gaylord saw the paper shake as his hands trembled. Then he sighed and passed it back. "Frank, I thank you kindly. But . . . under the circumstances, I can't take this."

"Why not? It would give you the start of a herd and—"

Clint laid it on the table. "Not unless you throw in with us. Until you do, this bill of sale and even the title to my land aren't worth the paper they're written on. Because no man can call a ranch or herd his own in Colter County as long as Chain ramrods the law."

"I'll guarantee your protection!" Gaylord flared. "Do you think I'd let Gruber—?"

"I'm sure you wouldn't. But"—Clint's brows arched— "do you think I could accept protection that don't extend to others? When Billy Dann has the same protection and every other little rancher—" He raised his hands, then dropped them. "That's why you've either got to run with us or I run against you."

Frank Gaylord looked around the room at all their faces. Again the anger—and the sadness. They were fools and they would break their hearts and maybe worse would happen . . . and there was no way he could stop them; none. "So be it," he said quietly, not even angry, only sad again.

"Frank." Carla took a step toward him.

"No, Mrs. Doane, let it ride," Fielding said, and she halted. "Well, thanks for listening to us, Gaylord."

"Welcome," Gaylord said. He went to the door and paused there, hand on the knob. "I know you don't want advice from me, none of you. But, Clint, I got some for you and Billy Dann. I met Morrell again this morning, learned he didn't leave the county. You won't believe me, I reckon, but he's trouble, bad trouble. And it seems to me you got enough already. If I was you I'd cut loose from him. I mean that."

Dann rose. "Is that a threat from Chain?"

"No," Gaylord said wearily. "Just some advice from a

man that don't want to see either one of you tangled up or hurt. Take it or leave it as you please." Then he went out.

Well, he thought, the choice was made, the lines drawn. He thought of Florence, and the heaviness within him lifted. There is no other way, I reckon, he told himself as he walked back to his office.

CHAPTER VII

With Charlie Crippled Deer, the Crow halfbreed tracker, in the lead, Frank Gaylord and a deputy named Leroy Jonas rode through a bitter twilight in the bleak and jumbled hills at the county's southern corner. October: the wind had a knife-edge chill; the sky was the color of a bullet; a few random flakes of snow swirled and danced. Gaylord and his men had been in the saddle almost since daybreak, and men and horses alike were dead beat. There was, on top of that, the possibility of an ambush, and, leaving sign reading to Crippled Deer, Gaylord forced himself to stay alert, eyes probing each draw, cut, and gulch ahead, each grove of scrubby, thirsty juniper, and, in between, raking the skyline. Nevertheless, despite his weariness and the cold, he felt good. It was a relief to be out of Warshield, away from the turmoil of politics and people, the conflicting loyalties that pulled him this way and that. The last four weeks had been the most bitter and confusing of his life; he was almost grateful to the horse thieves whose trail Crippled Deer was following, for an excuse to leave all that behind. Out here, things were simple, clear-cut. This was what he was trained and paid for, why he wore a badge. The law had been broken; it was his job to bring in the horse thieves and the stolen stock, and that was something he knew how to do.

There were three of them, and they had counted on no

one missing the fifteen or twenty head for days; it had
been their bad luck that the driver of a Chain supply
wagon bound for a line camp had spotted them driving
the rustled animals hell-for-leather south. By the time
Gaylord had been notified, Chain men were already on
their trail. Now, as Charlie read the sign, they were
strung out all across this end of the county—the rustlers
still pushing the Chain horses hard, making for the county
line, the Chain pursuers following, and Gaylord and his
men bringing up the rear.

One thing was certain, Gaylord had already realized.
The thieves were Colter County men. They knew these
badlands, knew the shortest route to the county line that
offered the best concealment and sufficient grass and
water for the stock. When he caught up with them he
would undoubtedly recognize every one of them. Likely—

Then he realized that Charlie Crippled Deer had
pulled up his mount and was sitting rigidly in the saddle,
head lifted, testing the wind. Gaylord spurred up beside
him and looked at him inquiringly. Then he caught it,
too: the faint tang of woodsmoke on the icy wind.

"Not far," Charlie said. "Them four Chain men, I
reckon. Not long since they passed this way."

"Maybe," Gaylord said. "We'll take no chances."

Crippled Deer nodded and swung down. "I'll scout
ahead." He handed Gaylord the reins.

"Whoever they are, be careful they don't see you,"
Gaylord said. "This light, you might git shot."

Charlie's copper face grinned tightly. "They won't see
me."

Gaylord and Jonas swung down in a cutbank's lee,
loosened cinches to let the horses breathe, and rolled ciga-
rettes. Part of Gaylord's mind remained alert, aware of

every sound and shift of wind and motion of grass or tree or swirl of dust; the rest of it ran back over the events of the past four weeks, after he had stalked out of Carla Doane's kitchen.

He had not really believed that they could do it. First they had to capture the Democratic precinct meetings to elect their own delegates to the county convention. Then, at the convention, if they had enough delegates, they would have to force through Clint Wallace's nomination over Gaylord's own. And, to begin with, there were only four precincts in the county. Chain Ranch was one, and Sir Randolph Hart's British-American Grazing Company, the second big ranch in Colter County, was another. That left only Warshield and the little village of Spear Creek, over on the west side of the county. Of course Gruber and Hart had locked up both the Democratic and Republican precinct meetings on their ranges; they voted the same men at each. Spear Creek was insignificant, only a handful of voters. That left Warshield, the pivot precinct. And surely he, Gruber, and Hart swung enough influence there to beat down any challenge in the Democratic meeting; there was no question about the Republican one; it was already theirs.

Still, Gruber and Hart had to be warned, and Clint defeated, for his own sake and for the county's. When Gruber had heard the news his face had darkened. "Why, the insolence of those damned rustlers! Well, we'll teach 'em a lesson they'll remember to their dying days!" He had turned on Gaylord. "You realize there's no way I can show your friend Wallace any special consideration after this! He's made his bed and now he'll have to lie in it!"

Gaylord met his eyes. "Gruber. There's one thing we'd better get straight here and now. I'll stand for no rough stuff where Wallace is concerned. Absolutely none. I don't intend to let him whip me in any election, but we'll beat him fair and square or you better find yourself another candidate."

Gruber's fists clenched. "Don't overstep yourself, Frank."

"That works two ways."

Then Gruber eased, laughed shortly. "Yes, of course it does. Don't get your hackles up, Frank. I'm edgy these days, anyhow. It's not an easy thing to make a ranch like this show a profit that'll keep its owners back in England happy—people who've never been here and don't understand conditions. Sometimes my nerves get a little raw." He nodded. "Of course. We won't need rough stuff, anyhow, to ruin their little scheme."

A week later the Republican precinct meetings were held; delegates backing Frank Gaylord for sheriff at the convention were elected without difficulty. Three days later came the Democratic meetings. Gaylord had been on hand for the one in Warshield, held in the Masonic Hall above Needham's Store.

He was startled. Usually only a handful of citizens attended such meetings; there had been thirty present at the gathering of Republicans. But now the hall was packed, overflowing, and people were still crowding on the stairs. Some, plenty, Gaylord recognized as Gruber's men, his own supporters. But there were others, the greasy-sack ranchers in their shabby denims and run-over boots, cowboys and drifters, some merchants and businessmen of the town—and, to Gaylord's astonishment, women. Led by Carla Doane and Joey Wallace, they were there by the dozens. He had forgotten that there were so many women in Colter County. But even the dance-hall girls and prostitutes from the saloons down the line showed up, in their best finery.

Fielding, Wallace, and Carla were among the first to come, and Fielding stalked up to Gaylord. "Well, do you believe me now?"

"How in the hell—"

Wallace said, "We told you, Frank. There are a lot of people fed up bad with Chain. They'll strike at Gruber— even if they have to do it through you."

"Yeah, but these women—"

Carla said very coolly, "Have you forgotten, Sheriff Gaylord? Women have the vote in Wyoming Territory. And Joey and I thought it was about time they started using it." She allowed herself an icy smile. "That's one thing Major Gruber overlooked—using women to solicit the women's vote. But we didn't."

"So I see," Gaylord said.

After that, it had been a knock-down-and-drag-out fight. Gruber's contingent put up a terrific battle, but they were swamped by the Fielding-Wallace forces. Even though a batch of Chain riders arrived, to vote here as well as in their own precinct on the ranch, they were too late to get in and turn the tide. Placed there deliberately by Fielding, a dozen women blocked the doorway to the jam-packed hall. Without using force, there was no way the Chain men could bull through—and force against the female sex was out of the question. Balked, they stalked out and headed for the saloons. The Fielding forces won a decisive victory, not only there but in Spear Creek too, which Gruber had ignored as not being large enough to matter.

"All right," Gruber rasped when he heard the news. "They've won a couple of precincts. The convention'll be

a different matter! Wallace is still a long way from getting
his name on the Democratic ticket!"

Maybe, Gaylord thought now, finishing his cigarette,
and maybe not. He and Jonas tightened their mounts'
cinches. One week from today, the convention would be
held in Warshield. And, no doubt about it, Fielding had
the delegates to dominate it. Gruber could not break it up
with rough stuff, even if he wanted to; half of Fielding's
people were women.

And that, Gaylord thought, hunkered against the chill
wind, was where Fielding had outsmarted them. Wyoming's charter was unique in giving women voting rights.
Until now they'd hardly used them, and had been no fac-
tor in Warshield or Colter County. But Fielding and
Carla had seen the opportunity and seized it. Gaylord
would not underestimate the lawyer again, and Gruber
would do well not to.

"Frank," Jonas said tautly.

A shadow moved in the dusk. "Charlie," a voice came
softly, and the halfbreed appeared from behind a clump
of boulders. He sniffled, dragged a hand across his nose.
"It's the Chain men, okay. Camped up the draw. That one
with a sawed-off and a face like he's been dead a
year—what's his name?"

"Lang," Gaylord said.

"Him and three others."

"How far ahead of us you reckon those horses are,
Charlie?"

Crippled Deer considered. "They passed this way four
hours ago; the Chain men, one."

"They been on the run ever since they lifted them
animals." Gaylord thought aloud. "They're likely almost
to the county line by now, but not quite. Those horses will

be dead beat, they got to rest and water. And they couldn't make any time through this country in the dark anyhow." He paused, in his mind unreeling a map of the county. "Bone Canyon, I expect. There's water there and grass, and it would be easy to hold the bunch. We got time. They won't travel again until the moon's up, at the earliest, and likely not before first light. Okay, let's mount and join up with Chain. Charlie, you lead the way."

Filing up the draw behind the halfbreed, Gaylord thoughtfully chewed a match. Gruber had not told him which men he'd dispatched after the thieves: he was not pleased to find Lang among them. The skull-faced gunman set his teeth on edge, the kind of man he'd have rousted long ago if he weren't on Chain's payroll. Gaylord had seen brass tacks, at least a dozen of them, driven in the shotgun's stock. It was not an affection he respected. Well, he would handle Lang—or send him back to Chain.

Crippled Deer drew rein. "They're over in that side draw, where it fans out in a holler."

"Right enough. You two stay here." Gaylord put his horse around the halfbreed and rode up the side draw. The taint of campfire smoke was strong in his nostrils; presently he saw the glow of flames. Pulling up his mount, he boomed: "Lang! It's Frank Gaylord!"

A moment's silence. Then Lang's voice came back to him, dry and raspy, the kind of voice a skull would have if one could talk. "Gaylord? All right, ride in slow, until we recognize you."

He put the sorrel forward toward the fire, saw, where the draw widened, the four men well away from the light, dark shapes standing tensely, and he knew that guns were trained on him.

"You see me now, Lang?"

"We see you. Come up, Gaylord."

He turned in the saddle and called to Jonas and Crippled Deer. Then he rode on into the firelight and dismounted. "Hello, Gaylord." Lang came forward, shotgun cradled in his arm's crook. "You know these others? Fisher, Harmon, Lightner?"

"Gentlemen," Gaylord said as Jonas and Crippled Deer rode in. "How's the coffee situation?"

"Enough left, I reckon." Lang, lean, almost skinny, in his middle thirties, turned to the fire and the light danced on hollow cheeks shadowed the sockets of deepset eyes. When it touched his pupils they gleamed with an odd, reddish light. Thin lips seemed never to quite close over big, yellow teeth. "That halfbreed better have his own cup."

"If he hasn't, he can drink out of mine," Gaylord said coldly. Jonas and Charlie dismounted, and the coffee was poured; Crippled Deer lacked a cup and Gaylord passed him his. "You made some time," he said to Lang.

"We'll get 'em tomorrow," Lang said.

"No. Tonight. Tomorrow they'll be across the county line."

"County line. What difference does that make?"

"Plenty, to me," Gaylord said. "They cross the line, I have no jurisdiction."

Lang's lips peeled back in a ghastly grin. "This has jurisdiction everywhere," he said, touching the shotgun barrels.

Gaylord did not answer. Instead, he went to his horse and opened a saddlebag. The metal stars he took from it gleamed in the firelight as he turned, holding them cradled in one big palm. "All right," he said, "line up here. All four of you."

Lang looked at the stars. "We don't need that tin."

"You wear this tin or you head back to Chain," Gaylord said.

Lang straightened up. "Not if it means we got to stop at the county line."

Gaylord ignored that. "Raise your right hands and repeat after me. . . ."

Lang sucked in breath. "Now, you listen, Gaylord—"

"No, you listen," Gaylord said. His eyes raked the four men coldly. The other three were no petunia blossoms, he thought, but they were not in Lang's class. "I am the sheriff of this county and I'm deputizing the bunch of you. Once you pin on that star, you take my orders or I'll have your hide. You don't want to wear it, you get out now. Make up your minds."

Lang stared at him, lips peeled back from teeth. Then he grinned crookedly, a ghastly twist of mouth. Slowly he raised his right hand. "All right. Whatever happens, it's up to you to straighten it out with Gruber."

"Repeat after me," Gaylord said, ignoring that. " 'I, whatever your name is, do solemnly swear . . .' "

They mumbled it. He handed them the badges and watched while they pinned them on. "Now," he said. "Fifteen minutes. Then we put out that fire and ride."

"You're the boss," said Lang, but his eyes were hard and there was mockery in his voice.

———————

Gaylord led them, with Charlie right behind and Jonas bringing up the rear. It was not a matter of trailing, now, but of instinct and knowledge. Long years behind a badge had taught him to think like a variety of wild and dangerous men: he could put himself in the boots of rustlers, highwaymen, bank robbers, and horse thieves. In the first place, these stock lifters should still have no idea that they were being trailed; secondly, they had pushed their stolen horseflesh to the limits of its endurance. And in the third place, they obviously knew the country, and Bone Canyon was probably where they had been heading all along. A gamble, but all the pieces fit, so it was as close to a sure thing as he needed. They could make some time and reach Bone Canyon by two hours after midnight. That was just right, for at that time of morning the human spirit—and a man's alertness—was at its lowest ebb. He remembered how he and Clint had hit Dann and Hoff at that time . . . and then put the memory from his mind. To wipe it out he thought of Florence.

He had kept his promise to her; he had been at Chain every free moment to see her. And she had kept hers to him; she had come to Warshield every week. And the door to that whole new world Gaylord had glimpsed that first night at Chain had now swung wide. There had been long rides together, alone, and the pleasure of showing her his country. And there had been endless talking, and more than talking; there was passion beneath that sweet exterior, a passion that drew her to his arms and had her returning his kisses with what was almost wantonness. They understood and knew each other now, and Gaylord could see a dazzling future stretching before him: Sheriff Gaylord and his wife, later, maybe, Congressman Gaylord and his lady. Even, perhaps, Governor Gaylord, with Florence by his side . . . A heady dream for a man not used to dreaming, but one now within his grasp, almost. First, of course, he had to get reelected. Without that he was nothing; without his badge he had reached a dead end. And he was not without rivals, either; Hart, the young Englishman, had his eye on her. "But really," Florence had laughed. "He's so effete, so effeminate—compared to you." And then, eyes kindling, smile fading, lips parting: "Kiss me again, Frank."

Governor Gaylord. No, it was not beyond possibility. Neither was a big ranch, with the right backing, and some sons and daughters with yellow hair. . . . Hell, Gaylord thought, with a woman like that, the sky's the limit. A man would be a fool not to shoot as high as he can reach. . . . Then he reined in, and so did Charlie Crippled Deer. Because both of them had recognized an overhang of rock: they were nearing the entrance to Bone Canyon.

"Charlie," Gaylord said.

The one word was all the half-Crow needed; he was off his horse in an instant, scuttling up a ridge, crouched low, making no sound at all, quickly lost in darkness. The others waited, without words. Gaylord was thinking of the canyon's shape, like a buttonhole, narrow entrance, narrow exit, swag in the middle. Lang started to roll a cigarette, but Gaylord seized his bony hand. "No fire," he said. "No light."

It seemed, there in the cold darkness, like an eternity, but in reality only twenty minutes passed before Crippled Deer materialized from nowhere. "Jesus," Lang said, swinging up his shotgun as the man appeared.

But Gaylord blocked him off. "Well?"

Charlie was panting slightly. "They're there, all right. Got both ends roped off and they're sound asleep."

"Okay," Gaylord said. "Charlie, you guide Jonas and Lightner to the north end, block it, and take cover. Drop Harmon on the west rim as you go. I'll put Fisher on the east. Lang and I'll block the south end. When you've put

down your man, give your coyote yap, just loud enough
for us to hear it. Then we'll move in from each end. You
men on the rim, you cover us, but don't you open fire
unless they do. You're just our insurance. The idea's to
surprise 'em while they sleep, and take 'em alive. I'll have
the ass, every scrap of it, of any man who opens fire
before they do or I do. That understood?"

"Good Christ, Gaylord," Lang snapped. "If they're
asleep, we can shoot the bunch—"

Gaylord turned on him. "You hear what I said? They go
in alive to face a judge. You shoot before I tell you to,
you'll face one, too. And I'll swear out the warrant."

"Gruber—" Lang began.

"Can't save you, and he won't, if I'm after you," Gaylord said. "Now, you understand? We're not out here to
tally brass tacks for that greener."

"All right," Lang grated finally.

"Charlie, move out," Gaylord said.

He waited until Crippled Deer and his men were gone.
"You stay here," he told Lang, and he and Fisher went on
foot in darkness. Gaylord got him to the heights on the
east rim and stationed him in good cover behind a rock-
burst. "You lay doggo unless they resist. Got it?"

"You're the boss," Fisher said, and Gaylord scuttled off.
His body ached with weariness as he silently descended
to the canyon mouth, but he ignored it, except to think:
Clint would still be fresh and rarin'. . . . Maybe, after all,
it was a job for a younger man. Then he thought of Clint
trying to deal with Lang, and he shook his head. No. Clint
lacked a wad, yet, of having what it took to run Colter
County. . . .

"Lang," he whispered. "Gaylord. Coming in."

"All right."

He joined the skull-faced man in the cover of a bend of the canyon's mouth. "Now we wait," he said.

Lang whispered an obscenity.

Gaylord crouched there by him in the darkness, yearning for a cigarette, feeling the tension that always came before the risk. But when he moved out he would be all right. Meanwhile, he was conscious of Lang's smell. He himself stank, after his long ride, but Lang's odor was worse, that of someone long unwashed, a kind of rotting smell.

Time passed. The moon was long since up but clouds veiled it nearly totally. Downcanyon, Gaylord heard horses almost too tired to graze. Their own were tied far enough away, with the wind right, so that neither they nor the bunch in the canyon would catch each other's scent and give alarm.

Waiting was part of it, always had been. That was how you took your men alive. Damn, did Lang never bathe?

Then it came, the yapp-yurr of a coyote, from three quarters of a mile away, wholly authentic. But Gaylord recognized it for what it was. His pulses hammered. Now. Time to move out.

"Let's go," he whispered. "And remember, hold your fire unless they shoot or I do."

He held his Winchester at low port as, slightly crouched, he moved forward, feeling his way for maximum silence. They passed through the narrow canyon mouth and entered the loop of the buttonhole. Gaylord saw the glow of fire embers, like a red star fallen to earth, three hundred yards ahead. Men exhausted by a long, grueling day would lie around it in their blankets. Dead to the world, easy meat.

He cast a glance to his right, at Lang. The man had

fighting savvy, all right. Like a wraith, shotgun raised, he seemed to drift over the ground. And now the fire was only two hundred yards away. There was plenty of time. Ten minutes to cover the next hundred and fifty. Down-canyon, horses snorted, shifted, one neighed: Charlie Crippled Deer and Jonas were coming through them.

By the fire, a form lifted, a man coming up under blankets, propped on his elbows. The horse downcanyon whickered again. "What—" Gaylord heard the mumbled word, saw the body twist, fumbling—maybe for a weapon.

He ran forward. "Don't move!" he roared. "You're covered, all of you! Hands up! It's the law, Frank Gaylord speaking!"

Jonas snapped, from the other side, fifty yards away, "You heard the man! Stand fast! First bad break and you're dead!"

Jonas, Gaylord thought, had the stuff. He'd make a sheriff someday. His voice was right.

The awakened man froze, then turned his head, his face a white blotch in the darkness. "Gaylord?" he said groggily. And now the other two were sitting up. "It's Gaylord," the first man said. "Boys, he's got us cold. For God's sake, don't drag iron."

And then, that simply, it was over. And yet it was not simple at all, Gaylord thought: only seemingly so because he and Charlie knew the country and he knew his business. A man who knew his business always made hard things look easy.

"Charlie," he said, "build up the fire."

The halfbreed piled the wood they'd gathered onto the embers. Meanwhile, Jonas warily collected guns. "Sheriff," he said, "near as I can tell, they're slick."

"We'll see. On your feet, you men. Hands on your heads. Face the fire. I'll shoot the first one breaks bad."

In the firelight, they staggered out of bedding, still stunned and groggy, and Gaylord felt a kind of sadness. He knew one of them, Tully Wyatt. Short and heavyset, a Chain rider last year: he stood out in Gaylord's mind because he carried a banjo with him everywhere he went and played it superbly at the least excuse. He had been in demand for dances last year. "For God's sake . . . Tully!"

"It's me, I'm afeared, Frank." Wyatt's voice was dull and heavy.

"Who're these other two?"

"Henderson and Wilson," Lang rasped before Wyatt could answer. "Chain men, too, until last summer."

They were hardly more than kids, Gaylord thought. Still, he was thoroughly professional as he shook them down, checking cuffs, backs of waistbands and, boot-tops for knives. But they were slick, all right. A pistol each, and one rifle among them, comprised their armament.

"Goddamnit, I never have no luck," Tully Wyatt said. Greedily he drank his second cup of coffee. "I'd've sworn it would have been a week before anybody even knew those hawses was gone. But that blasted wagon—"

"Tully," said Gaylord. "You oughta have known better anyhow."

Dawn was near now, the sky streaked with gray. "Maybe," Tully Wyatt said. Then he laughed bitterly. "Anyhow, I got a square meal out of it. That's more than me and the other boys have had since God knows when. Since Chain blacklisted us, anyhow."

"Blacklisted you," Gaylord said. He leaned against his

saddle, rifle cradled in his lap. Physically, he felt a sense
of well-being: it had turned out that the rustlers had neither coffee nor food; they had not eaten all day. But
Gaylord's men and the Chain riders were well supplied: a
big meal had been cooked and then cleaned up by everybody, rustlers and lawmen alike. The horse thieves' weapons were stacked well out of reach; anyhow, Gaylord had
sized them up as not dangerous. Three young cowboys,
none of them as old as Clint . . . and now years in prison
faced them.

Well, that was how it went, and you trained yourself to
quench any feelings about it you might have. "What do
you mean?" he went on. "Blacklisted?"

"Hell, Sheriff, you know," said Henderson, whose four-
day beard was mostly pale fuzz. "Or maybe you don't.
You never had to work for thirty a month and scant and
greasy found like us."

"I've served my time lookin' at a cow's rump," Gaylord
said.

"Not for an outfit like that Chain," Wyatt snapped, and
his round face had lost its good humor. "Anyhow, it was
the food that got us blacklisted. Spring roundup last year,
and all the other wagons was eating good. Take Hart's
outfit for example, you could bang the coffeepot anytime
you took a notion, and there was pie once a day. But
Chain? Good Christ A'mighty! Day in, day out, beef and
beans. Same thing three times a day, the whole roundup.
And that's where me and Woodie Henderson and Larry
Wilson got crosswise. Major Gruber rode out one day, and
we braced him. Goddamnit, all we wanted was pie like
the other outfits got; we thought he didn't know what was
goin' on and would set it right. I mean, your friend Lang

there was wagon boss, and Lang don't eat nothin' anyhow. So we thought we'd take our bitch to the major."

"Go on," said Gaylord.

"Well, there ain't no more," Wyatt said. "He clouded up
and rained all over us. If we didn't like the chuck, we
could haul our freight! He paid us off then and there, like
we was slaves or dawgs or somethin', and chased us out of
camp. Okay, to hell with him. Plenty of other outfits need
riders at roundup time. Well, we have wandered all over
Wyomin'. And there ain't a job to be had, not the minute
we let our names loose. I mean, it took a while to sink in,
but then we had it. Somebody had laid the black-ass on
us. Well, by God, we damned near starved. We would've,
if it hadn't been for my ol' banjo! I picked up a buck here,
a buck there, to keep us through the summer playin' it.
Then we tried the fall roundup."

His small, red-lipped mouth twisted. "Same old story.
We was dead, only we wouldn't lay down. We tried to
ride the grubline, but there warn't no grubline. And after
a while we got tired of havin' our bellybuttons up against
our backbones. I knowed where the Chain horses run, and
we figured Chain owed us somethin'. So, okay. We lifted
eighteen head. Figured we could get away with it. Well,
we figured wrong." He spat out cold coffee between his
cracked, run-over boots. "We can't fare no worse in Rawlins than we have so far."

Gaylord said, "Damn it, Tully, you could have come to
me. If you'd asked me, I'd have found you somethin'."

"We talked about it," Wyatt said. "But then we decided
you were Gruber's man as much as Lang is. And no point
in wastin' time bendin' your ear; you'da told us the same
thing Gruber did: If you don't like it here, go somewhere
else." His eyes suddenly blazed. "And, goddamnit, I like it

here! And when I come to Wyomin' I didn't know I'd have to kiss Ross Gruber's behind, and the association's, to stay here! Looks to me like a man oughta be able to make a livin' in this country without kissin' Gruber's butt! But—" His mouth warped again. "But you wouldn't know about that, Sheriff."

Gaylord snapped: "That's enough, Tully! Now, you three roll your sugans! We're headin' back to Warshield! Charlie, you and the others bring in the saddle stock and round up those loose horses. Jonas, you and Lang keep an eye on the prisoners."

Lang lifted his shotgun. "Yeah. All right, you waddies snap to it. And the first man breaks, he collects nine buck!"

As the prisoners began to roll their blankets Gaylord turned to the fire, poured the dregs of the coffeepot on it, and began to kick dirt over it.

And then the shotgun roared.

In the narrow canyon its sound was thunderous.

Gaylord whirled, Colt in hand, then froze.

What had been Tully Wyatt lay sprawled on the ground, only a red mess now, nearly cut in two by the blast of the open-bore ten-gauge. Larry Wilson lay groaning nearby, his right pants leg turning red.

"Lang!" Gaylord bellowed. "Goddamn you!" He took a step forward, Colt raised like a club, and Lang spun on him, teeth bared.

"Stand fast, Sheriff! You want the other barrels?" Gaylord heard the rasp of his breathing. "That bastard had a gun cached in his bedroll. He was draggin' for it when I let him have it!"

"A gun?" Gaylord turned. Impossible. He'd checked their gear himself. Then he saw it, propped against a saddle beneath a blanket. Covered like that, it could have been a draped and hidden Winchester. But it was not.

Gaylord snarled a despairing curse. He strode to Tully's bedroll, threw back the blanket, straightened, and faced Lang with flaring eyes. "His banjo!" he rasped. "It wasn't a damned thing but the poor kid's banjo!"

Lang's gaze shuttled to the instrument leaning against the saddle. For a moment even he looked shaken. Then his mouth twisted in a warped grin. "Well, his bad luck he reached for it without takin' that blanket off of it. What the hell, I saved the territory a pile of money!"

Jonas was already cutting away the cloth around Wilson's wound, as Henderson stood there pale-faced. "He took one buck in his leg," Jonas said. "Ain't too bad."

Gaylord nodded, never looking away from Lang. "All right," he said. He holstered his Colt and held out his hand. "The riot gun, Lang. Give it here."

Lang's eyes had a reddish glow. He held the weapon with its barrel centered on Frank Gaylord's belly. "No, sir. Nobody takes my shotgun."

"I do," Gaylord said. "You're my deputy and you killed this man in the line of duty. That'll save you from Rawlins yourself. But you used bad judgment and I'll not have it repeated. I want your riot gun and your other irons."

Lang did not answer. "That's an order," Gaylord said. "Jonas, if he shoots me, you and Charlie burn him down." He stepped forward, and Lang tensed, but Gaylord did not interrupt the smooth motion in which he seized the shotgun barrels and swung them aside. He and Lang locked eyes, and then Gaylord pulled and Lang released his grip. Gaylord broke the weapon, withdrew the live shell, and rammed it in his pocket. "Now the handgun."

Lang made no attempt to mask his hatred as he passed it over. "This ain't finished, Gaylord."

"It had better be," Gaylord answered calmly. "Charlie, rig two travois, one for the body and one for Wilson. Larry, I'm sorry. I don't reckon that helps you, and it sure don't help Tully. But you should never have touched those horses." Suddenly he felt it, all of it, the riding, the sleeplessness, the strain, and the anger and the sickness lying in his belly like a huge lump of something poisoned and undigested. But none of it showed outwardly as he went about the business of getting his prisoners, the body, and the stolen horses underway to Warshield.

CHAPTER VIII

That weariness and sickness seemed to linger even after he was back in town, and there was only one medicine for it: Florence Gruber.

Three days later, riding with her across the Chain range, he felt it all peel away from him, the heaviness, the sense of being somehow smeared with something foul. It was a fine morning, and she was a superb sidesaddle rider, mounted on a small, blooded black gelding; in red velvet riding habit, sun glinting on blond hair, she was something to take away a man's breath. And once more it was all worth it, especially when they stopped to water their horses in a grove of cottonwoods by a little creek.

She came into his arms naturally, as if it were where she belonged, and held up her mouth for his kiss. "Ah, Frank," she said at last when she pulled away. She walked to the stream's edge, and looked at the clear, running water. He came to stand beside her. Presently she said, very quietly, "Where do we go from here?"

"I know where I want to go."

She looked obliquely at him, blue eyes half lidded. "Do you?"

"Yes. And you know, too."

She did not answer, but turned her gaze to the stream again. "After the election I should be going back to Philadelphia."

Gaylord smiled faintly. "Do you want to?"

She laughed softly. "Not really. Philadelphia will seem awfully small and dull after Wyoming. And . . ." again, that oblique glance, "lonely."

"Then don't go back," Gaylord said. "Stay here."

She turned. "Frank, is this a proposal?"

"You know it is." Something clogged his throat. "Yes. I want you to marry me, Florence." Words rushed out, then. "I haven't got much now, no, not a lot to offer you. But if I get reelected, and I aim to, I'm not going to stop with being sheriff of Colter County. I used to think that was all there was. But now I've raised my sights. I've got plans of my own, Flo, big plans. You might think they're crazy, but—" He broke off.

"No. No, I don't think they're crazy. Neither does Ross. He has plans for you, too; you know that. He believes in you. So do I. And . . . it pleases me to see how much you believe in yourself and us."

"You're saying yes, then." Gaylord took a step toward her.

She held up her hand. "I can't say yes until you've talked to Ross, Frank. I guess I'm old-fashioned, but . . . he's head of the family now, and I'm dependent on him, and . . . I know he thinks the world of you. Talk to him first; then ask me again."

Gaylord stood motionlessly. "If he says yes—?"

She smiled, and the way it lit her face almost made him dizzy. "I think you know what I'll say then." She turned away. "Now, let's ride back to Chain. He'll be in this morning, and you can speak to him."

"Come in, Frank." Gruber rose from behind his office desk. "You and Florence have a nice ride?"

"Fine one, Ross." Gaylord looked at the squat, powerful man, with his square, brown face, piercing eyes, and broken nose. He felt a strange surge of resentment. All his life he had been a free man, making his own choices, his own decisions. But now his future rested in this man's hands. Major Ross Gruber held the key to everything he wanted to make his life complete. And for the first time Gaylord felt the necessity of pleasing someone else, of having to curb his own will, like a wild horse tamed to a strange hand. And yet there was no help for it. Not, at least, until he was reelected and he and Florence were married.

"Good." Gruber smiled, took two cigars from a humidor, and passed one to Gaylord. They lit up. "Ross," said Gaylord, "I want to talk to you."

The major looked quizzically at him. "Florence."

"Yes. I want to marry her. She says I've got to ask your permission. Well, I'm asking it."

For a moment smoke veiled Gruber's face. Then he took the cigar from his mouth and his expression was revealed. Actually, there was no expression at all.

"Frank," he said, "that puts me between a rock and a hard place."

He turned over the correspondence he'd been reading, went to the window, and stood there for a moment, looking out. "Florence is my only kin," he said at last. "Myself, I've never married. Wouldn't inflict the life of an officer's lady on any woman. So she's all I've got, all I'll ever have, I suppose. A responsibility that's borne down on me for years." Falling silent, he opened the window and the fresh autumn breeze, warm for this time of year, filled the room and riffled the papers on his desk. "She's sought after, you know. She could marry well, very well, in Philadelphia."

Gaylord said nothing, touched with fear by Gruber's tone.

Then the major turned. "And yet," he said, "given a choice between Philadelphia and Wyoming, I'd rather see her stay here in Wyoming. Where I am, close to me. And I would like to see her marry a Wyoming man. But one of consequence, you understand. Florence is not a pioneer woman. She's not like your friend Wallace's wife, where even a soddy on the prairie seems a blessing after a life of sin in a dance hall. She's ambitious, and she likes society. . . ."

Then, surprisingly, he laughed. "Don't look so woebegone, Frank. I'm not saying no." He sobered. "But I am saying wait."

"Wait?" Gaylord echoed.

"Wait until you're reelected." Now Gruber's voice was crisp. "I think you and Florence would make a good pair. I have plans for you both. But I can't put those plans in train until you're reelected—and not just barely, but by a whopping majority. Once you're sheriff of Colter County again, the rest of it falls into place. With the Wyoming Stock Growers Association, and the Cheyenne Club, the people who draw the water here. But if you don't make sheriff again, if you let Wallace beat you out—" He paused. "Then what would you be? What would you have to offer her?"

Gaylord drew in breath. "Not much," he said. "All the same . . ."

"No, not much. So, let's leave it at this: I would be happy to see my sister marry the sheriff of Colter County, a man with a grand future ahead of him. But I couldn't give my consent to her marrying an unemployed man with no future. Therefore, I can't answer you until after the election."

"Damn it, Ross, the election's no problem. I'll win. . . ."

"Will you?" Gruber picked up his cigar again and relit it. "I don't know, Frank. The rustlers are powerful in this county. And Wallace has their backing. If he's nominated at the Democratic county convention, if he gets his name on the ticket, then you're in real trouble."

"He'll be nominated," Gaylord said, "but I can still beat him, fair and square."

"Can you?" Gruber fixed him with cold, dark eyes. "I'm not so sure, Frank. I think what we should do is head off his nomination. I think we should make sure you are nominated on the Democratic ticket as well as the Republican one."

"Well, that won't happen," Gaylord said. "I ain't got a chance. Clint's got the delegates from Warshield and Spear Creek. Chain and Wagon Rod can't beat him out. He's a cinch for the Democratic nomination. But, damn it all, I'll whip him in the election."

"No," Gruber said flatly. "That's a chance I don't want to take. I don't want Wallace's name on the Democratic ticket. I want him frozen out completely."

He dropped into the chair behind his desk. "I can see now where I made a bad mistake—and so did you. Chain and Wagon Rod's got enough delegates to offset the ones from Warshield. But Spear Creek could turn the balance in the rustlers' favor if those delegates are allowed to vote."

"No way you can stop 'em," Gaylord said thinly.

Gruber smiled. "Leave that to me. They got a long way

to come to Warshield. A lot of things could happen to delay 'em until the convention's past."

"No," Garlord said flatly.

Gruber's brows drew together.

"They've been elected legally, they'll vote for their nominee legally in the Masonic Hall day after tomorrow. Let Clint be nominated if they want him. I'll see he doesn't win the badge. I know how to campaign for public office."

"Maybe." Gruber's voice rasped with his displeasure. "All the same . . ."

"I'm telling you," said Gaylord, "that's one thing I won't stand for."

Gruber loooked at him for a moment. "Frank, don't get foul of me. Remember, a lot hangs on this election for a lot of people. Me, you, and . . . Florence." His mouth twisted. "You may be a good campaigner. But we don't have any women on our side—and meanwhile, that Doane female and that saloon girl that Wallace married are recruiting women voters all over Colter County. This crazy business of giving women the vote here can ruin us; overlooking it's another mistake we made."

"Maybe. But what I said stands. The Spear Creek people ain't to be hindered."

Gruber's eyes flared with rage, sudden, almost insane in its intensity; and Gaylord remembered all at once a story he'd heard about the man not long after he'd come to Warshield. Somebody in a bar had told it: *He tried usin' a spade bit on a colt that was hackamore broke. He ruined its mouth, and after a while it would just come apart, do nothin' but buck the minute he hit the saddle. He liked that, liked to show off. But one day he got thrown. And then it was like he'd gone crazy. He didn't even get up off*

*the ground, jest pulled his gun and shot the horse then
and there. . . .*

And in that instant Gaylord saw how deep ran the
streak of violence in Gruber, how fierce his pride and self-
will. For a clocktick, he thought that Gruber would come
across the desk. But then it passed; the Chain manager
drew in a long breath. "Have it your way, Frank. But—"
He broke off as someone hammered on his office door.
"Yes?"

"Lang, boss. Need to see you a minute. Right away."

"All right. Excuse me, Frank." Gruber, jaw set, rose and
went out of the room.

Lang. Well, there was nothing he could do about Lang,
either, Gaylord thought. No way to hold him for the
shooting of Tully Wyatt, so he was back doing business at
the same old stand, shotgun and all. Gaylord rose and
paced the room. Damn it, how had things gone so wrong,
everything gotten twisted up? Then he halted as the
wind, gusting suddenly through the open window, lifted
papers from Gruber's desk and dropped them on the floor.
Gaylord stooped, picked them up, and laid them back on
Gruber's desk. As he did, the contents of the one on top
leaped out at him in copperplate script:

. . . *my associates and I most disturbed about latest
balance sheet. We are considering personal inspection of
your operation in near future at a time of our choosing.
While we understand that present market conditions are
poor* . . . Then the door opened and before he stepped
back he just had time to see that the letter was headed
London, England, and signed "Swain."

"Now, where were we?" Gruber said. "Yes. One last
time—you still object to Chain's handling the Spear
Creek delegates?"

"I won't have it."

Gruber shrugged. "I guess that's it, then. After the election we'll talk some more about Florence."

Gaylord held his own temper in check with effort. For that matter, if Florence would have him—and he knew that she would—Gruber couldn't balk their marriage. But let that ride for now, play it easy. Don't push the issue. Likely that letter from his bosses already had the Chain manager in a foul mood. "Okay. I'll see you in Warshield at the convention then, night after next?"

"I'll be there," said Gruber. "At the head of the Chain delegation."

They shook hands and Gaylord went out. Florence met him in the corridor, eyes wide with question. "What did he say?"

Evenly, Gaylord told her; and she looked downcast. "So it all depends on that silly election." Then she brightened, pushed her body against his. "Well, you'll just have to win it, won't you, darling?"

Gaylord smiled. "I aim to," he said and kissed her.

After a long goodbye she let him out. On the veranda Lang lounged against a post, yellow teeth clamped on a match, shotgun cradled in his arm. He did not speak, but followed Gaylord with hard, reddish eyes as the sheriff unhitched and mounted.

Gaylord ignored him. He had plenty of other things to think about as he rode back to Warshield.

━━━━━◆━━━━━

This was a hard land, and life on it for all but a few was drab and brutal. Cowboys and little ranchers alike worked from dawn to dusk, risking life and limb on half-broken, iron-jawed horses; the former for a dollar a day, beef and beans, and a place to spread their blankets; the latter sometimes for even less. Even town merchants had to scrabble with worry-knotted bellies, competing for scarce trade and scarcer dollars. If a man was out of work or went broke, or when he grew old or got crippled up, he could expect no pension and little charity, less, probably, than a favorite saddle horse past its working years. You made it or you didn't, free to get rich, free to starve.

But the real enemy was the land itself, vast, magnificent, and contemptuous of the puny humans daring to try to tame it and wring from it a living. It expressed its scorn in merciless ways: searing summer heat, bone-numbing winter cold, and a wind that hardly ever stopped, rasping nerves with its ceaseless gusting. But the cruelest thing of all was the sheer size of Wyoming Territory, the great empty reaches of it, where loneliness was as much a part of life as breath itself, monotony a mean, subtle thing that could erode the mind and spirit as the wind ground down a bluff or butte. If you lived alone out there in the emptiness for too long, Wyoming could drive you mad.

And so they seized at any break in the drab and dusty pattern of experience, cowhands, ranchers, merchants, miners, railroad men, and farmers. A schoolhouse dance was worth a journey of five dozen miles each way, or a dogfight, or a hanging, or anything offering change, excitement. But, every two years, election time was the best of all, better than circus, county fair, execution, and payday Saturday night rolled into one. Because an election lasted longer, offered more fodder for argument and conversation, gave a man something to think about besides the wind, the weather, and his debts. Elections engaged the passions, the emotions, and they were serious business from start to finish. And that was why, even though the Democratic convention in Colter County was only a preliminary before the main event, the town of Warshield this chill evening was like an anthill through which someone had pushed a boot. It swarmed with people, every saloon went full blast, and there were lines at the free barrels of whiskey paid for by Chain Ranch, bearing signs: COURTESY OF FRANK GAYLORD!

For the first few hours the mood had been a festive one. But now, thought Gaylord, standing on the sidewalk outside Needham's Store, it had changed. It was growing taut, tense, ugly. He looked at the crowd milling around the entrance to the stairs leading to the Masonic Hall above, and he pulled out his watch. Five minutes until eight—the hour when the convention was due to start. And the delegates from Chain Ranch were here, and from Sir Randolph Hart's Wagon Rod. So, of course, were the ones from Warshield—yonder was Carla Doane, standing apart from the mob, engaged in whispered, apprehensive conversation with the lawyer, Fielding. But Clint and Joey Wallace had not appeared—and neither had the delegates from the settlement of Spear Creek, Clint's key supporters.

Gaylord bit his lip, and his gaze shuttled to Ross Gruber, standing with Lang and Sir Randolph Hart at the head of their combined delegations of thirty hardbitten cowboys. Gruber caught the look, smiled faintly around his cigar, and shrugged. He spoke to Hart; then, trailed by Lang, he sauntered over to Gaylord. "Looks like Wallace lost his nerve," he said.

Gaylord's voice was low. "Major, I warned you about interfering with the Spear Creek delegation."

The good humor seeped from Gruber's face. "So you

did. And I assure you, Sheriff"—his voice was crisp—"I have not done so. Wallace and his people are grown men. If they can't get here on time, that's their hard luck. Where's Judge Merkel?"

"Right here, Major." A dumpy man in a gray suit shoved through the throng, a key ring in his hand. Merkel, the district judge, held a federal appointment, but he knew who had gotten it for him—the association. He was Gruber's man; and he was also chairman of the Democratic party in Colter County.

"Way I make it, Judge," Gruber said, "in four more minutes you call this convention to order. Might as well unlock the door and let the people in. By the way, if I might make a suggestion . . . I think you should go directly to the nomination for county sheriff as the first order of business, tolerating no delay at all. The nomination should be approved by a majority of those delegates present and voting."

Merkel nodded a little apprehensively. "I'll try. But there'll be some hell raised."

"You're damned right there will be." Frank Gaylord's voice was harsh. "This convention's going to proceed in the usual way."

"Frank." Gruber's voice was scarcely more than a whisper. "Don't forget who your friends are."

"I'm not forgetting," Gaylord said. "But Clint Wallace is a friend of mine, too. We've had this out before, Major. I'm not afraid of facing him in a square election. And I aim to see he gets a fair shake on the nomination."

Gruber did not answer. "Judge, unlock the door and let's get on with it."

Merkel looked around apprehensively, took a step toward the door, then halted. "Judge!" Fielding's voice rang out above the mutter of the five or six dozen people gathered in the street and on the sidewalk. "One moment, please."

Then he and Carla Doane were coming up on the sidewalk before the store. Fielding's face was pale and grim, his eyes dark, intense. Lang stepped forward, shotgun in his arm's crook. "Major—?"

"Ease off," Gruber said. "Well, Fielding?" He removed his hat. "Mrs. Doane . . ."

"Judge," Fielding said, "as soon as you call the convention to order, I'll have several motions to present. These should precede any nominations."

"A play for time?" asked Gruber, with irony. "To give your late delegates a chance to be seated?"

"Normal proceedings of any convention," Fielding said. "First I'll request a reading of the minutes of the last meeting of the Democratic County Committee—"

"What you request and what Judge Merkel rules in order may be two different things," said Gruber. "Now, Judge, only a minute left. If you'll—"

"Major Gruber." Carla Doane stepped forward. She looked at Gaylord, and something in him clenched at the contempt burning in her eyes. Then she faced Ross Gruber. "Mr. Wallace and the Spear Creek people were due an hour ago. If they've been delayed, there's only one conclusion to be drawn. And I warn you now, sir, if those people have been harmed in any way—"

"Mrs. Doane, I take no responsibility for your delegates one way or the other," Gruber snapped, face reddening. "And I will not be threatened. Mr. Fielding may make his motions. Perhaps the judge will refer them to the delegates present. Perhaps they will be voted down. And—"

"And," Carla said bitterly, "Chain will take over the

convention and ramrod through Frank Gaylord's nomination. Then he can run on both tickets without any opposition." She whirled on Gaylord. "Is that the way you want
it, Frank?"

He could not help what stirred in him then as he looked
down at her: memory and regret. And however this came
out, he would not have her thinking that of him. He drew
in breath. "No," he said quietly. "It's not the way I want
it, and I've already told Ross Gruber that. Major," he
raised his head, to see Gruber looking at him fiercely, "I'll
have my say now. This convention will take its normal
course. There'll be no nominations made by anyone until
whatever preliminary motions that are made are considered. That ought to take about a half hour, I'd guess.
Maybe Wallace and the Spear Creek delegates will be
here by then. Anyhow, that's the way it ought to run—
and if it doesn't, I'll not let my name be entered for nomination on the Democratic ticket."

He heard Carla's sigh of relief, and saw the rage in
Gruber's eyes. But with no regrets he went on evenly: "If
Clint and the Spear Creek bunch aren't here by then,
there's nothing more we can do."

"Fair enough," Fielding said. "We have no quarrel with
that. Thanks, Gaylord. We'll ask no more."

"You wouldn't get it if you did," Gaylord answered
flatly. "You—" Then he broke off because he heard the
sound of riders coming. Beside him, Carla tensed and
raised her head.

Then someone shouted: "Spear Creek! It's Clint Wallace and Spear Creek comin' in!" And from the majority of
the crowd a ragged cheer went up.

"Thank God," Carla whispered. Gruber made a sound
in his throat. Now they had entered the main street of the

town, a dozen horsemen riding at the trot. All were armed, and Clint Wallace was at their head, flanked on one side by Billy Dann and on the other by Lew Morrell, the man from Texas. The crowd shifted, making way.

Hooves clopped, bit chains jingled, gear squeaked as the Spear Creek men rode up before Needham's Store. Clint Wallace reined in, lifting his hand in the signal to halt. His eyes swept the crowd and picked out Gruber, Gaylord, Carla, and Fielding. Then, eyes hard, Clint swung down, Dann and Morrell also dismounting.

Clint came forward, and the yellow light from the window of the saloon next door fell across the trio. Frank Gaylord drew in his breath. The former deputy's face was red and puffy, his cheeks smeared with black smudges almost like warpaint. His clothes were filthy, his left hand bandaged. Except for the bandage, Billy Dann and Lew Morrell were in the same condition—and so, Gaylord saw now, were the other Spear Creek men.

"Clint!" Carla's voice was full of fear. "What happened?"

Wallace ignored her, taking a step toward Gruber and Gaylord, on the sidewalk. The other two moved up beside him. Gaylord was aware of Lang, on the far side of Gruber, shifting stance. And now there was violence in the air, a bitter, acrid tang of it that he could almost taste, like the charged atmosphere before one of those terrible high-plains storms. Dann was unarmed, but Clint and Lew Morrell each wore two guns; and the light shone off the rifle barrels of weapons held by the other Spear Creek men, still mounted, looking down at the crowd.

Clint's voice was hoarse, weary, almost a whisper. His eyes, cold blue, full of rage, shuttled from Gruber to Gaylord, then back to the Chain man again.

"Well, Gruber," he said, "it didn't work. You did your best to stop us, but we got here anyhow. Now, stand aside. We're goin' in. Let's git this convention started."

There was, then, a moment of complete hush on the street of Warshield, save for the jingling of bit chains, the soft noise of a restless horse's hooves in the dust, as it sidled. Gruber stood there by Gaylord, thick, heavy, spraddle-legged, solid as a bull buffalo. "I don't know what you mean, Wallace." His voice was deep and steady.

Lew Morrell spat into the dust, then moved forward a pace or two, thumbs hooked in double, crisscrossed gun-belts. The holsters swung low, anchored with thongs around his thighs. His mackinaw was tattered; flesh showed through a strange, dark-edged hole in his Levis at the knee. "You don't know what we mean?" His tone was edged, mocking, and Gaylord heard the rage in it, controlled and, for that, all the more deadly. "It wasn't Chain, huh, that fired the grass in Pronghorn Coulee about four this afternoon?"

"Fired . . . Pronghorn Coulee? What are you men talking about?" Gruber was defiant. His voice held surprise, but its edge was tinny, and suddenly Frank Gaylord felt a coldness growing in him.

"Well, I'll tell you," Morrell said. "Clint's got a throat full of smoke, it hurts him to talk, so I'll do it for him. Just as we was fixin' to leave Spear Creek, half the damn prairie on the north side of town went up in flames. And the way the wind was blowin', it looked like burnin' out the whole settlement." He drew in a breath that made his barrel chest swell. "Every man jack at Spear Creek—and the kids and women, too—it took us all to git it out. If the wind hadn't changed, and that was a plumb miracle, we might not have. As it was, it held us up for hours, and we've damned near killed our hawses gittin' here."

"But we're here," said Billy Dann. "And we're gonna nominate the next sheriff of Colter County." He turned to Merkel. "Now, Judge, unlock that door and let's git on with it."

"Wait a minute." Gaylord stepped forward. "Let me get this straight—"

"There's nothing to get straight," Gruber said tautly. "They had a prairie fire at Spear Creek, it seems. They got it out and they made it here on time. All right. But I don't like the implication, Wallace. Fires are common in this kind of weather. You can't hold Chain responsible for an accident."

"Accident!" Gaylord could see that Morrell seethed with rage. "When a fire starts half a dozen places at once along a mile-wide front? Where I come from, we call it arson—and any sonofabitch that would burn out a whole settlement jest to rig an election—!" His voice choked off with fury, broken loose beyond control now; his hazel eyes were blazing. He stepped forward. "Gruber—"

"Wait!" Gaylord rasped, but he was too late.

"Lang," Gruber said, and suddenly the bodyguard was there, between Morrell and the manager of Chain.

"All right, Morrell—" Lang began, starting to tilt up the shotgun. "You—" He broke off.

It seemed that Morrell's hand had not moved, but the Colt in it, hammer eared back, was centered dead on Lang's belly. Even Gaylord gaped for a pair of seconds; he had never seen a faster draw.

Then the sheriff was acting instinctively, big hands up and spread, empty, as he placed his body between Lang and the muzzle of Morrell's gun. "Morrell," he said coldly. "Put it up."

Morrell's eyes met his, and their hazel depths still flamed. "Sheriff, don't you tempt me. You were in it, too. . . ."

"No," Gaylord said. "Put it up."

"Lew," Clint Wallace whispered, "you heard the sheriff."

Morrell hesitated. Then, very slowly, he pointed the Colt downward and eased the hammer. He replaced it in his holster. "But if that Chain lizard with the shotgun—"

"Clint, see Morrell stands fast." Without waiting for an answer, Gaylord pivoted. "All right, Lang," he said wearily. "Again . . . the shotgun. And this time you don't get it back."

"What?" Lang's eyes flared. "I told you before—"

Gruber said harshly: "Lang, let me have the shotgun."

Lang turned on him. "Gawd's sake, Major! Listen—"

"That's an order," Gruber said, with absolute firmness.

After a long second Lang, lips thin, passed the gun to Gruber, who broke it and handed the shells to Gaylord. "I'll be responsible for this."

"I don't want to see him carrying it off of Chain range again," Gaylord said.

"He won't. Now, I suggest we cease this nonsense and get about our business. It's past the appointed time for the convention to start. Judge, open up, if you please."

Merkel unlocked the door with a trembling hand. Gruber said, "Chain, follow me. Sir Randolph, are you coming?"

That broke the tension. Gaylord stepped aside as the Chain and Wagon Rod men filed past. The men from Spear Creek swung down wearily and hitched their horses. "You fellows go ahead," Clint Wallace said. "Morrell, you cinch your temper and watch your step. Billy, you take it easy, too. Fielding, Carla, I'll be along directly."

"All right. Come on, Carla." Fielding led her up the stairs.

Presently only Gaylord and Clint Wallace remained on the sidewalk. Clint turned to the sheriff. "Frank, you really believe Chain didn't have that fire set to slow us up and make us miss the nominations?" His voice was hoarse, strained.

Gaylord hesitated. "You find me proof that he did, I'll put him under the jail, and you know it."

Clint looked gravely at him. Then his weary face split in a smile. "Yeah, I know that. Don't get me wrong, Frank. I don't think you had anything to do with that fire. But . . ." He licked puffed, cracked lips, and when he went on his voice was pleading. "Frank, listen. It ain't too late. That offer I made in Carla's kitchen still holds good. You could stand up there tonight and refuse to accept Chain's support and join up with us and . . . I would be mighty proud to serve under you again."

For a moment Gaylord felt the temptation. Then he looked down at the badge on his coat. Deftly he detached it and tossed it in his palm. "I told you, Clint, it can't be done. This badge . . . nobody in Colter County's gonna wear it without Chain and Wagon Rod's backing. It ain't a question of seeing it on me or you. It's a question of seeing it on me or somebody like Tom Lang. Whose chest you want to see it on?"

"And I tell you, we can elect you without either Gruber or Hart."

Gaylord shook his head. "That's a chance I won't take.

For my own sake . . . and for the county's." *And for Florence's,* he added mentally. But his decision was unshakable; it could be no other way, and Clint read that in his face.

"All right," he said at last. "But remember this: you run with the goats long enough, you're bound to wind up smellin' like a billy, too. I aim to fight you, Frank."

Gaylord grinned; and then he could not help it, he squeezed Clint's arm. "Do your damnedest, son. If we got to have a race, we'll make it a stomp-down good one. And may the best man win."

Clint smiled faintly. "Then let her rip," he whispered, and he climbed the stairs ahead of Gaylord.

CHAPTER IX

Frank Gaylord was almost relieved when, as had been foreseen, Clint Wallace took the Democratic nomination for sheriff by a margin of four delegates. Now the air was clear, battle lines drawn; and Gaylord, a fighting man all his life, never entered into combat, physical or political, except to win. And, he told himself, he would win back his badge, too; he had no intention of letting Gruber, Hart, or anyone else take credit for the victory he vowed to achieve. It would be his; he would get himself reelected by a margin that would stun not only Clint, Carla, and their people, but Gruber and the association ranchers, too.

Because, Gaylord thought grimly, it was time to let all of them see who had the power. Not just Gruber, not just Hart, but the people in Cheyenne as well. By God, he would bring in the biggest, broadest majority ever racked up in Colter County, maybe in Wyoming, Clint or no Clint, and when that badge was on his chest for four more years, he'd run his county as he saw fit, not as Ross Gruber wanted it. And when he went to Gruber for the hand of Florence, it would be as an equal, a man of consequence, who had clearly demonstrated his own massive strength.

Typically, he carried the battle straight to the heart of Clint's home territory, Spear Creek. An hour after dawn on the morning following the convention, he was in Pronghorn Coulee with Charlie Crippled Deer, investigating the prairie fire. Gaylord's face shadowed as he looked across the vast burn toward the little settlement of sundried frame houses not far away. If the fire had reached them, Spear Creek would have become a torch, general store, saloon, blacksmith shop, and all going up in smoke, along with their owners' hopes and fortunes. That thought twisted his gut; if this was arson and he could find the firebug, he'd see him put away for years.

But neither he nor Crippled Deer found any sign that the blaze had been set deliberately. The prairie hay had been horse-belly high and as dry as tinder; a traveling grubline rider careless with match, then cigarette butt, could have set it along a wide front and ridden on without knowing what he had done. It had to be left at that, Gaylord thought with relief; he was about to ride down to town and make sure that everyone knew he had been here and done his best when he saw the horseman galloping across the burn.

Gaylord rode to meet him, stiffening in the saddle as he recognized Lew Morrell.

They met in the center of the burn, reining up their mounts. In daylight, Gaylord could see that the Texas man's face was mottled with burns and blisters, where sparks had landed. They made him no prettier nor less vicious-looking. "Gaylord," Morrell said challengingly. "What you doing here?"

"It's my county; I'm the law—remember?"

Morrell grinned. "Not for long." Then he was sober. "Clint and I already searched. There ain't no evidence we could find. But I still say it was Gruber's work."

"You and Clint . . . You're mighty thick." Gaylord looked at him with narrowed eyes. Again Morrell wore two tied-down guns; everything about the man clashed

with Gaylord's lawman's instincts. "All right," he said.
"Suppose you tell me why you've dealt yourself in to this,
Morrell. You drift in here, take up with Billy Dann, then
latch on to Clint. I put up with it at first, but you tote
more hardware every time I see you. You're the kind I
generally roust. I think it's about time you account for
yourself."

Morrell sat very straight, both hands laid on the saddle
horn, his eyes like chips of glass. "You roust Lang," he
said quietly, "and I'll go on my own. Otherwise, far as
you're concerned, Sheriff, I'm on the payroll of the
Ranchers and Cowboys Political Committee. Steady job,
workin' for our candidate."

"As what?"

"Let's say I watch his back," Morrell answered evenly.

"And let's say you're also an organizer for the Knights
of Labor," Gaylord said. "Here to stir up a cowboy strike."

"If I was," Morrell said, "I'd sure as hell want another
sheriff rulin' the roost here besides Frank Gaylord. One
that would give the cowboys an even break if they stood
up for their rights."

"And maybe that's not what you are at all," Gaylord
went on. "I never met a labor organizer, but I've met a lot
of gunhawks. I know one when I see him."

Morrell's singed brows raised sarcastically. "That a
fact? Well, I reckon it takes one to know one. And maybe
a gunhawk's what Clint needs if he aims to stay alive long
enough to wear a badge. Anyhow, I'll give you some advice, Sheriff. If you're aimin' to ride down to Spear Creek,
save yourself the trouble. We've got it locked up solid."

"We'll see," said Gaylord. "It's my county; I go where I
please."

"Suit yourself," Morrell answered, shrugging. He wheeled his horse and galloped toward the town.

At a slower pace, Gaylord and Charlie Crippled Deer followed. But the moment they entered the settlement's single street, Gaylord knew that Morrell had spoken truth. Wallace posters and signs were everywhere, and he could feel the hostility of the people. Clint himself awaited Gaylord outside the general store.

"Frank," he said, with a lopsided smile. His voice was still a husky whisper. "Light. I'll buy the coffee."

"Good," said Gaylord. "I want to talk to you alone."

———————

"You think I'm a fool?" Clint whispered across the table in the shabby little restaurant. "Sure, I know he's a hard-case." That warped smile again. "I sent a wire to the rangers down in Texas. He's clean with them, not in their Blue Book." The smile went away. "He's played it straight with us so far, a hundred per cent. Chain's long on his kind and so is Wagon Rod; our committee's short on men like him. Me, I'm glad to have him at my back." His eyes were cool. "Don't try to roust him, Frank."

"I would have long ago if he hadn't laid claim to your friendship. Me, I think he's using that friendship to hide behind." Gaylord sipped his coffee. "Listen, boy, I've been around longer than you and Fielding put together. Men like Morrell don't throw in with folks like you and Dann and the rest outa pure love for law and order. And you sure ain't payin' him fightin' wages. So he's playin' some kind of game of his own. My guess is, for the Knights of Labor."

"I wouldn't know," Clint said. "All I know is, he's a damned good man to have around. He's helped us build

our home place, and he watches over Joey when I ain't
around and he's like he was her big brother. These days,
that's a load off my mind. He says he's been stepped on by
the big boys down in Texas in his time and he knows
what we're up against. The way things are, I ain't about
to run him off—and if you try it yourself, you better be
ready to deal with me."

"Time I decide to roust him," Gaylord said thinly, "I'll
roust him, check with nobody." Then he eased. "Clint, I'm
just talkin' for your own good. These union organizers—they're every bit as tough as Gruber, and as
coldblooded. If he's one of 'em, he'll use you for everything he can; but if the time comes when you get in his
way, he'll turn against you like a rattlesnake. I'm telling
you this: You watch him, and you watch him close."

"It won't wash, Frank." Disgust settled on Clint's face.
"Damn it, play your cards fair and square. I know you
want to be sheriff so bad it gripes your bowels; you're
on the gravy train and you're scared to death I'll pitch you
off! But this is pretty lousy, spreadin' this kind of poison
among friends. Tryin' to divide us, make us distrust each
other." He stood up. "Next you'll be spoutin' stuff about
Joey or maybe Carla. I never thought you'd come to this,
but I reckon that yellerheaded hunk of fluff at Chain has
got you where it hurts. Now I'll say this one time, no
more: I trust Lew Morrell. I trust him as much as I ever
trusted anybody in my life except Joey and . . ." his voice
faltered "the old Frank Gaylord I used to know. Well, I
don't know where that old Frank Gaylord went. Damn it,
I wish I did. But meanwhile here's the gospel for you. You
worry about that shotgun man out at Chain, Tom Lang, if
it's gunmen that bother you. I'll take responsibility for
Lew Morrell!"

Gaylord rose, swallowing his rage. "It's your funeral," he said thinly. "But keep your mouth off of Florence Gruber, you hear? And—" He drew in breath. "I'll give you one more piece of advice, take it or not. Until you're damned sure you know what game Morrell is playin', you better have somebody watch your back-watcher!"

"I'll worry about my back," Clint whispered, "thank you kindly."

Gaylord threw money on the table. "All right, kid. I'll buy the coffee." He looked at Clint for a moment, his anger ebbing. "Incidentally, that smoke you sucked in's played hell with your voice. How you aim to campaign when you can't talk?"

"I'll talk soon enough. Meantime, I got people to talk for me. Joey, for instance. And Fielding. Don't you worry about me." He grinned tautly. "Just cover your ass, Frank—because I'm comin' after it."

"Anytime you're man enough," Gaylord said. He stalked out to where Charlie Crippled Deer waited with the horses; and by the time they were back in Warshield there was no more anger in him. But there was fear, plenty of it—for Clint Wallace. He spent the rest of the day writing telegrams, and had them all on the wire by nightfall.

————

And now the gloves were off, both forces electioneering at full throttle. If Clint wanted it, he'd get it. Gaylord campaigned with all his wit and strength on two fronts simultaneously.

First a string of barbecues and rallies held in Warshield and strategic points across the county. Chain supplied the beef, beer, booze, the fiddler and the banjo picker; Gaylord joined Gruber's other hand-picked candidates—for territorial legislature, county surveyor, assessor, and the like—on the speaker's platform. Everything was laid on lavishly, including the kind of spreadeagle oratory the voters loved to hear, and every rally was jammed and overflowing. Squire Hamp Melton, candidate for Territorial House of Representatives, carried the burden of the speechifying, a man who could really make the eagle scream. Later, Gaylord himself talked briefly, plainly, making the same promises about strict, fair, even-handed law enforcement he'd used from the beginning of his career. In the past, his manner and the simplicity of his talk and bearing had always been effective. Now, though, things were going sour.

The first rally, held in Warshield, set the pattern for the others. "And now, good folks of Colter County," Melton roared, "I give you a man you all know and respect, a man with decades of experience in law enforcement, a man devoid of fear, a man of fairness, honor, courage! I give you that paragon of Wyoming lawmen, Sheriff Frank Gaylord!"

There were cheers, but as Gaylord rose, coming to the lectern, they were drowned by boos and catcalls. "Ladies, gentlemen!" Squire Melton bellowed. "If you please . . ."

"That's all right, Squire," Gaylord said grimly. "I can wait."

He stood there patiently, and finally his big presence dominated the crowd that jammed the street. Meanwhile, he swept it with his eyes. Yes. There was Fielding, and Billy Dann, and there was Carla. His gaze met hers; she did not drop her eyes; Gaylord turned his face away. Women, he thought, more women than he had ever in his whole career seen at a campaign rally. Women from ranches, town, saloons, decent and shady, all rubbing shoulders, mingling, and . . . it gave the crowd a different temper, one with which he was not used to dealing.

Finally there was silence. Gaylord said in a deep voice that carried: "I'm not sure I deserve all those nice things Squire Melton said about me, but—"

"You sure's hell don't!" a man's voice shouted.

"But," Gaylord went on inexorably, "I will say this: I have done my best to enforce the law in Colter County without fear or favor. I have tried to keep this county clean. And I think I have done it as well as any lawman could. Moreover, I have experience—more than twenty years' experience as a county sheriff. I was ramrodding the law in Kansas when my honorable opponent was still learning his ABCs. I think you all know me and you know my record. And it's on that record that I stand or fall, on that record that I ask you good people to reelect me—"

"Don't ask us!" a woman's voice shrilled out. "Ask Chain Ranch!"

Another woman cried, "Those cattle Ross Gruber gave you free in your record? How do you explain that?"

"Gruber's bought you and you know it!" a female voice shrilled.

"And Clanton and Garrison, and half the bigwigs in Colter County!" a man shouted. Shouts of approval, boos, and the tumult rose.

Gaylord tried to speak, but it drowned his voice. "What about fear or favor?" somebody hollered. "We're afeared of bein' shot like poor Phil Hoff as a favor to Ross Gruber!"

"Shut your goddamn face!" a Gaylord man roared, and the crowd swirled, seethed. Fists were raised and a woman screamed, and Gaylord caught a glimpse of Carla

Doane, wearing an expression of half triumph, half anguish, that pierced him. There was no hope of being heard now, and in a moment there'd be fighting down there in that mob.

Gaylord whirled. "All right!" he roared at the musicians. "Play somethin'! And play it fast and loud!" The musicians broke into a thundering reel, and the music drowned the shouting and gradually calmed the crowd. By then Gaylord was off the platform and had disappeared, so the rest of the candidates could be heard.

Ross Gruber was furious, pacing the back room of Clanton's saloon, chewing an unlit cigar. Suddenly he halted, turned, took the stogie from his mouth, and gestured with it. "All right," he said harshly. "If that's their game, we can play it, too. From now on, Frank, by God, we'll have armed men at every rally. Let's see if they got the guts to carry on like that if it'll earn 'em a busted head!"

Gaylord stared at him. "You gonna bust the women's heads? They're the ones doing most of the carrying on." He poured himself another drink and stood up. "Don't be a fool, Major. If it was all men, we'd keep order, yeah. But nobody can keep order in a crowd of females."

"Let a few of 'em see their husbands catch a pistol barrel across the head," Gruber rasped, "and it'll quiet 'em down. And more than that. Wallace and his speakers get the same treatment at every rally *they* try to hold. Hart and I can have enough men there to break his parties up in a hurry!"

"And get somebody killed! Men like Wallace, Lew Morrell, Billy Dann, they won't take that lying down! No—"

Gruber went on as if he hadn't heard. "That's another thing. That saloon bitch that Wallace married. How long you think those women'll stick with Wallace when it sinks into 'em that half their men have probably slept with that slut one time or other?" He grinned. "From now on, we drag her through the mud at every rally. And I'll see the word gets spread—"

Gaylord said, in a tone that shut him off: "Major." Then he looked at the other two men in the room. "Sam, Herb, leave us alone a minute, huh?"

Looking at his face, Clanton and Garrison left without a word. When the door was shut behind them Gaylord turned on Gruber. "Major," he said thinly, "We'd better get some things straight."

After a moment Gruber said, "Yes. Yes, I think we'd better. Before this goes any further."

"All right," Gaylord said. "Here it is, and it's gospel. One: There ain't gonna be no bully-boys at our rallies. I'll not see any women get hurt in that kind of scuffle."

"They're asking for it—" Gruber began, but Frank Gaylord went on, overriding him.

"Two: You can put all the disturbers you want to at Wallace's rallies, but they don't break 'em up. No rough stuff. If there is, I'll arrest the whole kit and b'ilin'."

"Now wait—"

"Three: What Joey Wallace used to be will not be brought into this campaign in any way." Gaylord's voice rang like iron on iron. "You understand me? *Not in any way.*"

Gruber's face was red. "She was a—"

"I know what she was. So does Clint. She was what she had to be to stay alive. But what she *was* don't count. It's what she is now, and what she's gonna be."

Silent for a moment, Gruber said finally, "Frank, what do you think Florence will think when she hears you're defending such a woman?"

"I can't help what she thinks," Gaylord said. "I reckon it will offend her. Maybe it offends you. But it ain't the way things work out here. Especially not for women—not so far, anyhow. Maybe it will be different when we've got as many as they have in the East. But right now women like Joey are about the only kind there are that ain't already married. So if a man wants a wife, he takes one of those and he tries to forget and so does she. Clint and Joey are doin' a good job at that. Other people are willin' to go along. There's a song, Ross: 'What Was Your Name in the States?' It's about people that start fresh out here. That's one thing about Wyomin': Your luck went sour somewhere else, you can start over and nobody'll crowd you. So—"

"The hell with that," Gruber rasped. "She's going to be up there on the platform, speaking for Wallace while his voice is gone. It's the perfect time to rub her nose in what she used to be—right in front of a crowd!"

"And have Clint Wallace come lookin' for me to call me out. And then I'll have to kill him—or he'll kill me. Which, if he does, you'll be the next on his list. No, I won't stand for that. Put all the loudmouths in at Clint's rallies you can git there. Screw 'em up as bad as he messed up mine. But no pistol-whippin', no gunplay—and especially no word spoken against Joey Wallace."

Gruber looked at him strangely. "That's your say, is it?"

"That's my say."

"All right. Now I'll have mine." Gruber fished in his pocket and drew out a few strips of cheap newsprint, long and narrow. "Look at those."

"Ballots," Gaylord said.

"That's right. Four so far. The regular Republican ticket; the association ticket, I control. Now, you see these other two? They were printed up by men who control better than two hundred votes apiece. They came to me and said, 'Carla Doane's offered us three hundred dollars to print Clint's name on our private tickets. You want to better that?'"

His mouth twisted. "I bettered it, all right, and it cost money. And, Frank, that's what you'd better understand. To get elected, it all comes down to money. Money for the rallies, money to buy the votes, money to do any damned thing that's needed. Carla Doane has got the money. Chain Ranch has got more of it. She can break herself backing Wallace, but we'll swamp her all the same."

He paused. "There's an old saying, Frank: *The man who pays the piper calls the tune*. Well, in your case, I'm paying the piper and I insist on calling the tune."

"Major—"

"You wait," Gruber said, and his eyes glittered. "Without Chain's money, you don't have a prayer of winning. Even with it, things can still go wrong. This election's important to me, damned important, and I'm not taking a chance of losing it and turning over control of this county to the rustlers. Now we'd better get this straight. You've got to make a choice. Either you go along with me or there'll be a new sheriff in Colter County, and his name won't be Frank Gaylord—or Clint Wallace, either."

"You're not making sense," Gaylord said. "All right, I need you, but you need me just as bad."

"No," Gruber said. "Don't fool yourself." He smiled faintly. "I want you, yes, but you can be replaced." He waved the ballots. "On every one of these tickets. It's a very simple matter. Chain owns the board of county commissioners. Chain could have them fire you tomorrow for inefficiency and appoint Tom Lang in your place. Then we'd have stickers made and paste in Lang's name over yours on all these ballots—perfectly legal, here in Wyoming. And you'd be out, Frank—out as sheriff, out as a lawman altogether when word got around you were fired for cause. And out with Florence, too, sad to say."

"Florence . . ." Gaylord said thickly.

"I'm her only living relative, her sole support. She does what I tell her to. Except for me, she'd starve—unless she married well. Marrying a jobless man with a ruined reputation wouldn't be marrying well. She loves you, Frank, but when push comes to shove, she'll do what I say. And I'd never let her marry a man with no prospects." He threw the chewed cigar into a spittoon. "Now, do we understand each other?"

"No," said Gaylord. "You don't understand me at all. You and your threats. Major, you don't scare me. I've been scared by experts. If that's the way you feel about it, you can take your badge and ram it, crosswise. I'll throw my support to Clint Wallace and ask him for a job as chief deputy."

Gruber stared at him. "You're crazy."

"No. I won't be threatened, not by anybody."

"And Florence . . . ?"

Gaylord drew in a long breath. "You said she loves me. And, God knows, I love her. I'll take my chances there." He unpinned his badge and held it out. "Here, you want it that bad, take it."

Gruber looked down at the star in Gaylord's big palm. His face worked. Then he smiled a little crookedly. "All right, Frank, you win. We'll compromise. We'll still break up Wallace's rallies, but no real rough stuff. And—we'll respect Mrs. Wallace's reputation." He raised his head. "Pin that badge back on."

"As long as we understand one another," Gaylord said.

"We do," Gruber said heavily. "We do."

———————

Frank Gaylord left that meeting with no sense of triumph, only a strange feeling of being dirty, smeared with something foul. Nevertheless, he had done the best he could. For his own sake, for Florence's, and for the county's. He had to win—the alternative, he knew now, was Tom Lang. For if Clint won, Gruber would find some way to oust him and install Lang behind the star. And with Lang and his shotgun ramrodding the law, no one except those allied with Gruber would be safe.

So he threw himself into the second phase of his campaign, and this went better—at first. Personal contact, long horseback journeys all across the county, stopping at every isolated homestead, ranch, and crossroads, one man to another. He was good at this; he liked, understood, people; and they sensed something in him to which, always before, they had responded with their trust—and votes. But as the campaign swirled on even this started going sour. Now he was met with a hostility that soured him.

"All right, Jud," he asked one little rancher as they squatted, chewing grass stems, before the man's log shanty, while his wife boiled clothes in an iron washpot in the yard. "We been friends a long time. I've done you some favors. Now you tell me you won't vote for me. Let's have it—why?"

Jud Tripp raised his weathered face. "Well, because I'm fed up, Frank." Rising from his squat, he went on: "I'm fed up with bein' pushed around by Chain. I'm fed up with the way you've run your campaign."

"The way I've—"

"Chain's hired gunmen breakin' up Wallace's meetin's, that kind of thing."

"Listen, Jud, have you seen what Wallace's people have done to mine?"

"That was women. They didn't move in with guns, lookin' like they was gonna use 'em at any minute. And—"

"And another thing," Mrs. Tripp cut in. "They didn't spread the kind of dirty talk about you and Carla Doane—though, God knows, they could've—like you and your folks have done about poor Joey Wallace." She came toward them, drying hands on her apron, and Gaylord faced her.

"I've spread no talk about Mrs. Wallace," he said thinly. "Who has?"

"I dunno who's behind it, but if it ain't you, who is it?" She looked at him with disgust. "We all know what she used to be. And me, I admire her for gittin' out of it, tryin' to lead a decent life. But the ugly talk that's goin' 'round is enough to turn a pig's stummick. . . ."

Gaylord said quietly, "It's none of my doin', Mrs. Tripp."

"Well, it's your people's doin'!" she flared. "And I'll tell you this, Sheriff—Wyomin's the only place in the whole United States of America where a woman can cast a vote. And me, I aim to cast mine for Clint Wallace. And my man, here, he better do the same, or he'll be hard put to find somebody to warm his feet at night!"

Tripp's mouth quirked. "You see the fix I'm in, Frank."

"I see," Gaylord said grimly. "Thanks for the explanation. Well, cast your vote to suit your conscience. It's a free country." He stalked away and swung up onto the sorrel.

There was no use, he thought, in bracing Gruber anymore. The major would only deny the whole thing. But the Tripp family's reaction was the last piece in a puzzle that until now had baffled Gaylord. And as he pounded back to Warshield he was struck with a sudden certainty.

He was going to lose.

Let Gruber buy his votes, let him spread his scandal, let him use his bully-boys. Frank Gaylord would not be reelected. A tide of revulsion—against Gruber, against Chain, against the association—was sweeping through the county, and it would wash him out with it. Maybe it would be close, but no matter what he did, no matter how many votes Gruber bought, Frank Gaylord was finished as sheriff of Colter County.

That he could accept. He could maybe find another job, elsewhere. But . . . Florence? Would it cost him Florence?

Only last night he'd held her in his arms and kissed her furiously, and she had returned his kisses with equal passion. She had said it last night: *Oh, Frank, I love you so much.* . . .

No, it would not cost him Florence. The hell with Gruber! They would marry and she would follow wherever he went, and somehow he would see to her and fulfill her desires and give her the life to which she was accustomed and make her happy. Anyhow, he knew how big-time politics worked now, and maybe in another state or territory . . .

He felt better. He could survive anything as long as he

had Florence, and he was sure of her. But meanwhile . . . well, he could not just roll over and play dead. He'd still give Clint a run for his money. And he'd make Gruber see how his tactics backfired.

Nevertheless, that certainty of defeat was still riding him when he reached Warshield. After stabling his horse he went to his office, where Callaway met him. "Everything's quiet, boss, but you got a mess of telegrams came in today."

Morrell. Gaylord went quickly to his desk and thumbed through them. Ranger headquarters at Austin; marshals and sheriffs at San Antonio, El Paso, and Dodge: all negative, no record on Lew Morrell . . . He shoved them aside, his puzzlement adding to his sense of impending disaster. Damn it, he knew a hired gun when he saw one, and that was what Morrell was, and Clint was betting the wrong horse, and . . . He began to write out a more detailed description of the man. He owed Clint that much, at least. There was something phony about Morrell, something as wrong as a nine-dollar bill. The man had wormed his way into the confidence of Clint and the little ranchers apparently for no profit. And that stank. Nobody did anything in this world anymore out of selflessness, idealism. Everybody was out for what he could get. Morrell wanted something, and whatever it was, it might cost Clint more than he could afford to pay.

Either way, Gaylord thought, rising to pour himself a cup of coffee, maybe the time had come for a showdown with Morrell. Clint would holler, but Gaylord wore the badge here, and that was that. Yeah, the time had come to roust him. And in the long run it would be for Clint's own good, his and Joey's safety.

He raised the cup of coffee to his lips. Then the door

loudly slammed open and Gaylord whirled, pouring hot liquid down his sleeve.

Terry Fielding stood there, powdered with dust, as if he'd ridden hard. The lawyer's lean young face was pale, his eyes great flares, and what seemed like tears had cut channels in the dust on his cheeks. "Gaylord," he whispered, his voice shaking. "Oh, godamnit, you were right and we were wrong. You warned us, you warned us about Lew Morrell. . . ."

"What?" Gaylord strode toward him.

Fielding leaned against the doorjamb as if exhausted. "Clint's dead," he said. "And Joey. And Billy Dann." His indrawn breath was a painful sob. "Lew Morrell has killed them all."

CHAPTER X

With the help of Morrell and Dann, the soddy had been completed. The interior of the little hut, hardly twelve by twelve, seemed too small for the three corpses sprawled grotesquely in its confines.

The body of Joey Wallace sat on the bed, slumped back against the earthen wall, wide-open eyes staring in shock and horror at the door across the room. She had been shot twice in the chest.

Billy Dann's corpse lay just inside the door, face down. Clint Wallace's lay just outside, staring at the sky. His right hand held a gun from which two rounds had been fired. The soddy reeked of blood and the other unsavory smells of death, which Gaylord knew all too well.

Looking down at Clint's lean face, smeared with scarlet that had poured from mouth and nostrils, he tried to remain impassive, but he had to swallow hot, stinging bile. "Christ," he said, and he pulled the blanket back over Clint and turned away. The wind was refreshing and cold; it helped; after a moment he was in possession of himself again. "All right," he said, surprised at the steadiness of his own voice. "Let's have it again."

Fielding had been sick beside the soddy. Now he wiped his mouth and managed words. "They were worn out from campaigning, especially Joey. Clint sent her home from the north end of the county to get some rest, sent Morrell with her to look after her."

Gaylord's eyes shuttled to the woman's body on the bed and he made a sound in his throat.

"Clint and Billy put in a full day of it and followed on. I hated to bother 'em, knowin' they needed a day of rest, but we'd picked up another bloc of votes and I thought they ought to know, so I rode out early this morning, and—they were like that when I found 'em. Only . . . Clint was still alive."

Fielding swallowed. "He died while I tried to help him. But he managed to say something. There was a lot of blood; mostly it was . . . a kind of gargle. But I caught two words. *Morrell*. And *Ten Sleep*." He paused. "Then he was finished. And I—I took a look around, but I didn't touch anything; it's all just like it was. Except that Morrell isn't here and he isn't at Billy Dann's and— You can see what happened."

"Yeah," Gaylord said. "I reckon."

"He . . . must have gone after Joey. And Clint and Billy walked in on him. And Morrell . . . I've seen him practice. He's hell with a gun. They were tired and surprised and— He could have taken 'em both."

"And those holes in Joey . . . ?"

"Morrell, to shut her up. Or—" Fielding broke off.

Gaylord looked at him steadily. "Or maybe it wasn't all Morrell," he said. "Maybe it was Joey, too. And Clint found 'em together and—"

"He wouldn't have," Fielding whispered. "To begin with, Joey wasn't like that. I know what she used to be. But she would have died before she hurt Clint—and he would have before he hurt her."

His voice steadied. "Anyhow, it was Morrell. However

it happened. Clint left no doubt of that. I would have known it anyhow. You have got to go after him, Sheriff. You have got to take the bastard and hang him."

"I figure on it," Gaylord said. He turned away, stared out across the bleak, rolling country of the basin at the distant smudge that was the Big Horns. The wind was turning colder, scraping at his face like a steel blade. The sky was lead-colored; pregnant with winter. Gaylord felt colder than the wind. Because now he knew, saw what he should have seen all along. He fought back the sick rage flaring in him. Surprised by how steady his own voice was, he said: "Ten Sleep, huh? At the foot of Powder River Pass, over the Big Horns. He's headin' for Johnson County, likely. When you get back to Warshield, tell Callaway to wire the sheriff in Buffalo to look out for him, hold him if he shows."

"Yes. Where are you going?"

Gaylord turned up the collar of his sheepskin coat. "To Ten Sleep, where else? But first I got to talk to Gruber." He stepped up into the saddle, and, looking down at Fielding, said: "Whoever it was, I'll see him hang. Bring in the bodies, please. See they get a decent burial. I'll stand good for all expenses." Then, touching the sorrel with his spurs, he sent it into a run.

———◆———

Gaylord dismounted, hitched the horse, went up the steps, and twisted the doorbell of the Chain Ranch house. Standing there, waiting, he felt as if all emotion save rage and grief were burnt out of him.

Florence Gruber swung the door wide, her beauty accentuated by a white dress foaming with lace. Her face lit. "Frank! How nice! I didn't—"

"No. Where's Ross?"

"In his office. But— Frank, is something wrong?"

"A lot," he grated. "Clint and Joey Wallace and Billy
Dann have all been murdered."

"Murdered?" Her eyes widened. "How ghastly." Then,
as surprise ebbed, she said, "But that means there's nobody to run against you. . . ."

Something in her voice rasped Gaylord's nerves. "It
means exactly that." He shoved past her, went to Gruber's
door, knocked, and entered.

Gruber, startled, looked up from his desk. "Well . . ."
He smiled. "An unexpected pleasure. Sit down, Frank,
have a drink."

"No," said Gaylord. He looked at that square, powerful
face with its broken nose, the heavy brows drawn together in a frown. The sight of Gruber sickened him. How
could he ever have admired the man?

He watched Gruber's eyes carefully as he spoke. "Clint
and Joey Wallace and Billy Dann are dead. It looks like
Lew Morrell tried to rape Joey and Clint caught him, and
he shot 'em all."

"My God . . ." Gruber rose. "This is awful." But Gaylord did not miss the tinny ring in his voice, the way his
eyes clouded to veil their true emotions; and Gaylord
knew. He had, he thought sickly, been right, dreadfully
right. "What happened?"

Carefully, Gaylord told him what he and Fielding had
found, and while Gruber was a good actor, smooth, he
was not good enough. It was there, behind the act.
"Well," Gruber said at last. "It's a sordid thing, but to be
expected with such people. After all, she was a slut. I suppose she led him on—"

"Ross," said Gaylord in a tone that quenched Gruber's speech.

The Chain manager stared at him.

"You had it done," Gaylord said.

Gruber's face, beneath its bluish cast of beard, paled. "Wait a minute, Frank. . . ."

"You saw it, didn't you? Just like I did. You've gone too far, turned everybody against Chain Ranch—and against me. You saw that Clint was bound to win. So you had him rubbed out." Gaylord drew in a breath. "Morrell was your man all along, wasn't he? A spy in the enemy camp. The whole thing was phony, the way he braced me in the saloon, badmouthed Florence in front of the town, forced me to fight him. . . . All that was your idea, eh? Put him on the inside, where, if it came to that, you could use him."

Now Gruber's face was even paler; his shock seemed genuine. "I think . . . you believe . . ."

"I believe you hired Morrell to spy on the little ranchers and told him to kill the Wallaces," Gaylord said thinly. "And I was a fool for not realizin' that sooner."

Gruber swallowed hard. "I told you to roust him, insisted, and you didn't. . . ."

"Part of the cover, too. But it doesn't matter. I'm going after Morrell. I know which way he headed—to Ten Sleep and over Powder River Pass. One way or the other, I will get him—and take him alive and make him talk. And if you had the Wallaces killed, Major Gruber, I will see you hang, along with the man who did the actual killing."

Gruber's mouth twisted. "You'll not talk to me like that."

"I'm just telling you," said Gaylord. He backed toward the door.

"Frank," Gruber said. He had recovered now, was smooth, steel under velvet once more. "Frank, wait a minute." He hesitated. "I'll give you my word Morrell is not my man. And I know how you feel; I know how close Wallace was to you. But we've got to be practical. The election is only five days away. You can't leave to trail Morrell over Powder River Pass or whatever right now. True, at the moment you don't have any opponent anymore, but Fielding's clever, there's no telling what he might do. And in the past few weeks he's gotten the Democratic party here in the palm of his hand. He might put up someone else to run against you, and if you're away on election day that could be serious."

He paused. "I sympathize with your grief, but we've got to take maximum advantage of this . . . ill wind. We've got to have time to iron out this misunderstanding, you and I, and muster our forces and make sure nothing goes wrong. It's a rotten thing to happen, but it's a break for you, and you've got to see it that way. I don't want you to leave Colter County before the election. I want you here campaigning every minute."

"No," said Gaylord.

"Wait. I don't mean Morrell goes free. I'll give you Lang and Withers. You deputize the pair of them and send them after him. Lang's the best and Withers is almost as good. They'll bring him in, one way or the other, justice will be satisfied, and—" He read Gaylord's eyes. "Don't be a hardheaded idiot, Frank. Your whole future's at stake."

Gaylord said quietly, "I'm going after Morrell. Not

Lang, not Withers, not any Chain man that can shut Morrell's mouth before he lays the blame where it belongs." He sucked in breath. "Me, myself, I'll take him alive. And when he talks, I'll be back to see you, Ross."

"Do you know what you are saying, Gaylord?" Gruber asked after a moment.

"I'm saying that I won't be sheriff if it means using the dead body of my friend as a stepping stone," Gaylord said. "I'm saying that you figured me almost right, but not quite, Ross. I was a hungry man, but not all that hungry. You misjudged me, Major." He put his hand on the doorknob.

Gruber said, "And you've misjudged me, Gaylord. I'll tell you something now. You have a choice. Stay here and send Lang and Withers and keep on being sheriff. Or go out that door after Morrell and lose everything. And I mean everything. Your badge, Florence, the works."

"Like I told you before," Gaylord said, "I've been scared by experts." Loathing Ross Gruber in that moment, he turned and went out. And almost bumped into Florence, who obviously had been listening at the door.

She jerked back, her face pale. "Frank, I heard— How dare you accuse my brother of such a thing?"

For a moment, as he looked down at her, Gaylord's resolve almost faltered. "Flo, I hope I'm wrong. But I got to find Morrell and learn the truth."

She seized his arms, pushed her body against his. "No, Frank. Please. Don't you know what this means? If you defy Ross, he won't let me marry you. . . ." Her voice thickened. He felt the pressure of her breasts on his chest. "What difference does it make about them anyway—a dance-hall floozy and a pair of rustlers? Don't you see,

Frank, what counts is *us!* Don't throw our whole future away for *them!"*

Gaylord felt a strange, cold sickness in his belly. "We wouldn't have much future if you can't understand why I got to go after Lew Morrell."

"Frank, I beg you—"

He had never thought it possible. But now he pushed her away from him, roughly, and she brought up against the far wall of the hall. "Leave off, Flo. Either you love me or you don't. Anyhow, I got to go."

She stared at him with lambent eyes, and her face changed; suddenly it was as if her brother's face were somehow there beneath the lovely mask. "All right," she husked. "Then go ahead. But"—she gestured toward the door—"if you walk out, don't you come back. You hear? Don't you come back to Florence Gruber and Chain Ranch! Go sleep with that slut you made up to before I came, that Doane woman!"

Gaylord stepped backward. "That's right," she hissed. "You think I didn't know? Well, everybody knows about Carla Doane! I was willing to forgive, but now— If you turn your back on Ross, you turn your back on me! And you'll never lay a finger on me again!"

It was strange. Gaylord, somehow, was not surprised. Sick with hurt, yes, but the grief he felt for Clint was so great that not even this could touch him. A pattern, he thought. Gruber never missed a bet to make a fool of me. And in that instant he no longer loved her, for he knew that she was as false as Lew Morrell. He said only, "All right, if that's how it's to be." And he turned and went to the front door.

As he opened it she screeched his name. *"Frank!"* But

he was already mounted and heading toward the Big
Horns.

———————————

He had a long way to go and a lot of time to think. Up-
permost in his mind was one imperative: get Morrell and
make him talk. But there was more, much more: Carla
Doane; Clint; himself; Gruber. And he began to see: he
had his share of guilt. Morrell, Gruber, whoever had
conspired in Clint and Joey's killing was not more guilty
than Gaylord himself. He was a conspirator, as well. Because if Gruber had not figured Gaylord as being his own
kind, Clint would still be alive. And Gruber had figured
right; he had been Gruber's own kind for too long. . . .

On the long ride he thought about his father, the old
lawman facing the Texas trailhands. He thought about all
the hard towns he had been in, and the bribes he had
been offered, and— A man got softer as he got older.
Maybe he was too old to hack it anymore. But no. He
could cut it until he found Morrell. After that, he would
have to stop and think about what the law was all about.

He pushed hard, and by mid-afternoon was out of his
jurisdiction, across the Colter County line. Still far away,
the Big Horns loomed, snow-capped, against a gunmetal
sky. Powder River Pass crossed them at ten thousand feet,
almost; there would be snow up there by now. Morrell
might count on that to blot his trail. Surely one thing he
had not counted on was Clint hanging on to life long
enough to say where he was bound. He figured that
Gaylord and Charlie Crippled Deer were still searching
slowly, painfully, for his trail.

So, with a good start, maybe he would not push. Maybe
he would even linger in Ten Sleep, and Gaylord could

catch him there. But Gaylord knew that that was a forlorn
hope. Morrell was a professional; he would be out of the
territory as soon as possible, maybe even out of the
country. Swing up through Montana or the Dakotas, and
then to Canada . . . Gaylord spurred his mount.

That night, in rough country, he halted only long
enough to let the horse rest and graze; then he rode on
through cold growing more bitter. Late sunrise found him
working through the upshelving land near the mouth of
Ten Sleep Canyon, and now the mountains towered over
him.

But the sorrel was dead beat, and it was mid-morning
before Gaylord rode into Ten Sleep, a cluster of buildings
along a single street at the end of a huge gorge cut by Ten
Sleep Creek. His rifle across his saddle bow, he scanned
the town alertly, despite his own fatigue, looking for the
dun horse Morrell would be riding—or for the man himself.

He saw nothing. He put the sorrel to the rack and entered the one cafe. Men looked curiously at the stranger
in the sheepskin coat, eyes circled with weariness, star on
his chest. At the counter, Gaylord ordered coffee, watching the door, and identified himself. His description of
Morrell was terse but clear. And when the counter man
nodded Gaylord's heartbeat quickened. Morrell had been
here; all right—and gone.

"He pulled out 'fore daylight this mornin'," said the
man behind the counter. "First customer I had. Spent the
night at the hotel, I think, then come here for breakfast.
Didn't talk much. I seen his kind before, thought somebody might be on his trail. So I watched which way he
went. He rode upcanyon."

Gaylord sat heavily on the stool. "Steak and eggs," he

said. "And rush 'em." He gulped the scalding coffee. So Morrell had four hours', maybe five, start up the climb toward the pass, thirty miles away. And his horse would be fresh and rested. When the food came Gaylord wolfed it down in five minutes, along with a second cup of java.

The town blacksmith dealt in horses and kept a corral and stables. Gaylord left the sorrel there and rented two sturdy, mountain-bred horses, packsaddle, and panniers. He bought grain, then, at the general store, food, cooking gear, extra matches, tobacco, and heavy Pendleton blankets. He had given Morrell another hour's lead, but only a fool would climb the Big Horns without the necessary equipment. It was nearing noon when he headed out of Ten Sleep, bound up the tremendous canyon for the pass.

It was a steep, hard climb, with the creek and sheer gorge walls on his right, high slopes clad with pine towering on his left. The wind whipping down from the mountains was like a blade of steel, and after an hour it began to snow, a thin, white dancing veil of it. Gaylord did not force the horses; he took time to scan the terrain ahead of him, scout every bend. Morrell was not the kind to forget to watch his backtrail.

Alert as he was, part of his mind was free to think about Florence Gruber. At first he had felt nothing, only a sort of numbness, like the shock after a sudden wound. Then, last night, riding through the darkness, there had been the pain. It had been rough, racking him as if wounded nerves had come back to life, but he had borne it. Now the worst of it was gone. What lingered was the memory of her furious face, so much like her brother's, her hissing, rasping voice. And such memories left no room for regret, only the strange relief that he had felt in the beginning. She had played her brother's game, all the way; he could see that now. And he did not hate her, could not, no more than he could think that she had ever really loved him. What she had loved was the picture Gruber had painted of Frank Gaylord's future: big, rich, powerful in Wyoming.

And maybe, he thought, he had not really loved her, either. Maybe he had needed someone to turn to after Carla, and she had been there, with all that blond, creamy loveliness. And there was no use crying over spilled milk. He was, perhaps, a lucky man. Then he grunted deep in his chest. But even there his luck had been bought by Clint and Joey's death. He touched his horse with his spurs, sent it up the grade a little faster.

By late afternoon he had worked out of the gorge. Now he was in a sloping country of meadows and thick pine forest. The snow was heavier, not quite a blizzard yet, but the lodgepole pines on the slopes were bending with a burden of white wetness. Wind and snow had wiped out all trace of Morrell's passing—but there was no other way for him to go. With his head start, he might be over the pass by nightfall; but he, Gaylord, would be lucky to make it before darkness settled in. And there was no chance of traveling at night up here in this weather. Already his hands and feet were icy, and he had bound the brim of his hat down over his ears with his bandanna. But, he told himself, he was, after all, enduring only what Wyoming cowboys hired through the winter were expected to suffer for a dollar a day and beans. Maybe, he thought, the Knights of Labor had a point; maybe a cowboy strike wouldn't be such a bad idea. . . .

Now it was getting darker; and as Gaylord crossed a wide meadow the wind took on a different sound. He raised his head and looked toward the crest, almost ob-

scured by driving snow. Up on the heights a blizzard
howled, and it would work its way down the mountains
soon. He had to get out of the open and find shelter in a
hurry. There would be no more traveling once the full
force of the storm hit him, and he needed a good place to
ride it out.

But, the thought struck him, for that matter, so did
Morrell. Maybe the storm up there would work to his advantage; maybe it would not only slow the fugitive, but
force him to turn back, run ahead of it and lose some of
the ground he'd gained. Gaylord, driven by a sense of urgency, forced the horses to move briskly into the wind.

Then he was off the meadow, in pine forest, and, despite the shelter, the wind was getting worse, the snow
driving harder. He had gone as far as possible, and he
turned all his attention now to finding a place to camp.

Then he saw exactly what he sought. To his right, a
vast pine forest spilled down the wooded slope. Its snow-
shrouded depths were divided by an outcrop of rock, a
kind of small escarpment, ranging from ten to thirty feet
in height, like a big, jagged step. It ran on as far as
Gaylord could see, vanishing in the woods. It was exactly
what he needed: the rock would reflect the heat of a fire
built before it and temper the wind against himself and
his animals. Gaylord rode into its lee, dismounted, and
tied the horses. They stamped gratefully in the shelter the
rock face provided.

He was off the trail far enough so that his fire would not
be seen. The first thing, of course, was to gather all the
wood he could lay his hands on—not fallen branches from
the ground, but squaw wood, dead, but still on the tree
and drier. He worked his way along the outcrop and
through the woods, breaking every branch within his

reach. He used the rock as guide and anchor, not daring to stray far from it; once out of sight of it, a man, in snow like this, could get turned around fifty yards from camp and die.

It was slow work, though, gathering wood. There was plenty of trees near the rock face, which seemed to go on for hundreds of yards, but for some reason not as much squaw wood as he'd expected. It was almost as if some other traveler had just harvested it. As if—

Gaylord halted and shook his head savagely. The cold, fatigue: they had numbed his wits. He was a fool, a goddamned careless fool. Did he think he was the only one who knew a place to make a blizzard camp when he saw it? Gaylord's heart began to pound. He dropped what wood he'd gathered, turned, slogged quickly back to his horses, and yanked his saddle carbine from its holster. He worked its action until he was sure it was free, then replaced the jacked-out rounds. Holding the gun with both gloved paws around the receiver, barrel tilted slightly down, he edged forward, in the shelter of the escarpment, back to where he'd left the wood. He passed that by, and now he shifted his grip on the carbine, round in chamber, and placed his finger on the trigger. Slowly, blinking away the snow that settled in his eye sockets, he made his stalk along the side of the rock face.

A hundred yards or so farther on, it bent sharply, almost at a right angle, away from Gaylord. He made no sound, was like a shadow in the swirling white as he worked his way toward that bend, then peered around it, looking down the line of the rock face until it vanished in the gloom of woods below. Then he tensed, and his breath went out in a little sigh.

There it was, hard by the shelf another hundred yards

down the mountainside: the orange flicker of a campfire barely visible through the driving veil of snow.

And now there was no more weariness in Gaylord, no fatigue, only an old, wild exultance he had often felt before, but never with such intensity—the lawman's knowledge that now he has his man.

Carefully, deliberately, he restrained the eagerness and rage surging up within him. He wanted Morrell alive, unharmed. Morrell had a lot of talking to do—and he would talk. Gaylord would see to that, alone with him out here in the wilderness of the Big Horns. Whatever it took, he was, just now, capable of doing.

With infinite patience he waited for it to get a little darker. Not much, just enough to mask his movements a little better, in case Morrell was sitting at an angle where he could watch his backtrail, the approaches to the fire. He thought Morrell would be; he did not underrate the man.

When Gaylord judged that the time was right he moved on, swinging out a little, taking shelter in the murk beneath the pines. The campfire grew in size, its blaze clearly visible now, as it was fed, gained strength. Gaylord changed his angle of approach, moving directly toward the orange light now. Then he was in position, behind a tree, directly opposite the fire. He saw it, built high and glowing brightly, and the blanket-wrapped figure huddled beneath the escarpment, big and bulky; no doubt about it, that was Lew Morrell. Gaylord's wind-blistered lips peeled back from his teeth in a wolfish grin.

Then he moved in to point-blank range. He lined the rifle on the figure, which, head down, laid another branch on the fire. The wind howled and whispered simultaneously in the pine woods. Gaylord's voice rose above it in a shout that rang and echoed. "Morrell!" he yelled. "This is Gaylord! Stand up and keep your hands high! You're covered, and you're under arrest, you sonofabitch, for the murder of Clint and Joey Wallace! And Billy Dann! And if you break, by God, I'll burn you down! Hands high and on your feet!"

A kind of shiver ran through the blanketed figure. Through the swirling snow, Gaylord saw it hesitate, then rise, arms outspread, blanket-draped, looking like a giant bat in the firelight.

Gaylord stepped forward, Winchester outthrust.

Then the man behind the fire raised his head.

"Whoever you are," he said in a voice with an accent Gaylord knew from the speech of Sir Randolph Hart, "please don't shoot. I assure you, I am not the man, Morrell. I am a traveler in a strange land and quite harmless."

Gaylord's jaw dropped. He shifted position; now, through the swirl, he could see that it was not Morrell nor anyone he had ever seen before, though the man was tall and lithe. This was a total stranger.

Something knotted within Frank Gaylord. "Who the hell are you?" he yelled hoarsely.

The wind dropped for a moment and Gaylord saw a long, weatherbeaten face, firelit. "My name is Swain, if you please, Mr. Gaylord. Lord Peter Swain, managing director of the British-Wyoming Land and Cattle Company, better known to you as Chain Ranch, perhaps. And I assure you I am innocent of any crime. I hope you will do me the favor of pointing that gun elsewhere. Because if you do not, my employee, Mr. Morrell, will most assuredly have to shoot you in the back."

Gaylord stiffened. "Your employee—"

"That's right," said Morrell, close behind him. As he

started to turn, the muzzle of a gun jammed hard against his spine, halting all movement. The gunbarrel twisted against the sheepskin coat. "Lew Morrell, Sheriff. And if you don't drop that rifle I'll kill you."

Gaylord stood rigidly.

"Drop it," Morrell repeated.

And Gaylord did.

CHAPTER XI

"You keep those hands up," Lew Morrell said, "until I git that Colt and belt knife."

Gaylord had no option, standing motionless as Morrell pulled his sidegun from its holster, then the Bowie, which he had bought in Ten Sleep. "Now," Morrell said, "down to the fire."

As they marched toward the blaze, the man who called himself Lord Peter Swain laid more wood on it. In the light of the flames swirling higher, a long, weatherbeaten face inset with bright blue eyes looked at Gaylord from under a black fur cap. Swain, Gaylord judged, was in his middle forties, and, even in this uncertain light, did not look like a man to be trifled with.

Swain asked crisply: "Have you taken all his weapons?"

"He's clean. But I'll keep him covered. He's hell on wheels."

"You may allow him to drop his hands."

"Put 'em down, Gaylord," Morrell said. "But I shoot at the first bad break."

As Gaylord lowered his hands Morrell stepped out from behind him and faced him across the fire, Colt leveled. "Now!" he yelled above the wind's howl, and his eyes glittered. "What was that you hollered about Clint and Joey? And why the hell you up here, stalkin' me like an elk?

Gruber find out about me and Lord Peter and send you to shoot us in the back?"

Gaylord said, "Clint and Joey and Billy Dann are dead, and you damn well know it. You tried to rape Joey and they caught you at it and you shot both of 'em and then killed her, too. And then fogged out. But you made one mistake. Somehow Clint knew you were bound for Ten Sleep, and he lived long enough to say it."

He was startled by the impact of his words on Lew Morrell. The man's face was suddenly stricken; he took a step backward, and the gun in his hand sagged off center. "You lie," he whispered. "Clint . . . Joey . . . dead? Billy, too?" Then he jerked up the gun, mouth twisting savagely. "Goddamn you, Gaylord, you'd better give it to me straight!"

Lord Peter Swain said, "Look here, you men. I don't understand this at all. Lew, watch him closely. Now, sir, tell me what you're about."

Morrell had recovered now. "Yeah, talk, Gaylord. Fast."

Tersely, Gaylord told them what had happened, watching Morrell intently. "It had to be you," he finished savagely. "You laid hands on Joey and Clint caught you at it. . . . Fielding told me you were there alone with her, and—"

"And you're a goddamned fool," Morrell rasped. "If you think I'd hurt Joey Wallace or Clint either . . . But—" His voice almost broke. "Gruber did a good job, didn't he? He saw his chance and took it—and pinned it on me."

Gaylord shook his head. "It won't wash, Morrell. It was Gruber had 'em killed, all right, but it was you who did the butcherin'. You've been his man all along, haven't you? He hired you to come in, get in with the little ranchers, do his killin' for him when he needed it—"

"Sheriff Gaylord," Swain, the Englishman, cut in sharply. "You are quite mistaken."

"Am I?" Gaylord turned on him.

"Indeed." Swain looked at him steadily. "I can assure you that Mr. Morrell did not kill anyone at any time in Colter County. He is a former Texas Ranger and a highly respected range detective under his real name, and he has been in my employ for several months. It was I who hired him and sent him to Colter County. And my orders to him were to make a thorough investigation of Ross Gruber and his management of Chain."

It was fully dark now; the wind had risen, howling through the pines like a spirit exiled from hell and heaven both; sparks flew upward, vanished.

Swain went on: "I'll try to make this brief, Sheriff. I don't want this misunderstanding to last one moment longer than necessary. . . . Our company has been most disappointed with Gruber's performance as manager of Chain. Losses in the past two years have been substantial. When Gruber persuaded us to go into this enterprise, he made bright promises; none has been kept. And now we have come to feel, my partners and I, that it is quite probable that Gruber has swindled us on an enormous scale—and that this was probably his intention all along."

His eyes flickered to Morrell, who held the gun steady. "He tried to justify these losses by claiming rampant cattle theft—I believe you call it rustling—by small ranchers and unemployed cowboys. There was, he said, no chance of a profit until this was brought under control, which he said, with the help of the Stock Growers Association and the local sheriff—you—he was working hard to do. Still, nothing seemed to get better. I wrote my friend Sir Randolph Hart to verify Gruber's statements; Sir Randolph replied that he had certain problems, but not of the magnitude that Gruber claimed. Still, as a stranger, he had to rely on Gruber's leadership and advice."

Swain paused. "That answer was unsatisfactory. On my first visit to Wyoming, when Chain was founded, I had met a rancher named Martin Shell, a most impressive man. I wrote to him in confidence, asking for his advice. His reply shocked me. Gruber, he said, was lying. There was minor rustling, but not on such a scale. Moreover, Gruber was spending a lot of money to make himself a big man in the association and in Wyoming, and he thought that he was a bad influence on both. He seemed to be deliberately making any reconciliation or agreement with the cowboys and the small ranchers impossible for everyone. And all of the territory would suffer the consequences if he kept on. . . . Would you like a cup of coffee, Sheriff?" Without waiting for an answer he poured one from a pot by the fire and handed it to Gaylord. The first swallow of its hot blackness revived him and he listened closely as Swain went on.

"My partners assigned to myself the responsibility to investigate this matter. We also have holdings in Texas, and Mr. Morrell had been helpful to us before. I retained him to come to Colter County and ascertain the true facts and then report to me. In the meantime, I voyaged to America myself, with the intention of first having Morrell's report, and then confronting Ross Gruber with it on a surprise inspection of Chain Ranch."

Gaylord remembered the letter in Gruber's office, the man's worry every time he spoke of the English owners.

"The quickest way to find out what was goin' on," Morrell put in, "was to win the confidence of the little ranchers. I did that by deliberately bad-mouthin' Gruber and pickin' a fight with you—Gruber's man. That put me on their side, they trusted me, and I knew if they were rustlin' I'd find out in a hurry. But there ain't any rustlin', Gaylord, nothing like what Gruber claims. A cow or two now and again for eatin' beef, not much more than that. Gruber's been stirrin' up trouble for some purpose of his own."

"Which has now become quite clear," Swain said. "I've talked in person with Mr. Shell. On a trip to the Dakotas, he picked up the information that Gruber has been in contact with a syndicate of Frenchmen who have holdings there. He has promised them that, for an interest in it, he could deliver Chain Ranch to them at a rock-bottom purchase price. Obviously his intention has been to discourage us and put us in a mood to cut our losses and sell out cheaply to the French. At the same time, though I have no proof as yet, I daresay he has used money siphoned from our profits to cement his own position in Wyoming. First, of course, to gain control over Colter County; then he would seek influence in Cheyenne itself. Once he had it, we, ignorant foreigners, would be in poor position to bring him to book. Gruber, in other words, has simply planned to climb to power at our expense. And, possibly, at yours." His voice was cutting. "Certainly, Mr. Morrell had no imaginable motive for killing your friends. Only Gruber could profit from such a murder."

"Or you, Gaylord," Morrell said coldly.

Gaylord stared at him for a moment, then drained the coffee cup. "No," he said. "You're not clear yet, Morrell. Bein' an ex-ranger and a cattle dick doesn't make you any sort of angel. You were alone in that soddy with Joey most of the afternoon, and maybe you figured, since she'd been a fast woman once, you'd take a chance. . . . Maybe Gruber's all you say. But the fact remains, Clint laid the blame on you."

Morrell said evenly: "How?"

"I told you. His last words to Fielding were: 'Morrell . . . Ten Sleep.'"

Morrell's mouth twisted. "Because he couldn't trust *you* to square with Gruber for him," he said contemptuously. "Don't you see? He was telling Fielding to find *me* and say what had happened." Morrell sucked in breath. "Just that morning I had a letter Fielding brought me from Lord Peter, here. Said he wanted me to meet him in Ten Sleep last night, that he was comin' over from Buffalo in Johnson County. Okay, I went home with Joey to their soddy and stayed with her until Clint and Billy came. But I didn't lay a finger on her, I guarantee you. And then the four of us had a drink, and I told Clint I'd be gone a day or two, had business in Ten Sleep, would be there if he needed me. And then I pulled out." He turned to Swain. "Hand me a cup of that stuff."

Swain poured a cup of coffee. Morrell went on, his voice bitter: "Meanwhile, I reckon, Gruber had made up his mind. You didn't stand a chance of beatin' Clint, so Clint had to go, and it didn't matter if Joey and Billy went with him. Somebody must have been watchin', saw me pull out, then moved in and killed 'em all. Rigged it to lay the blame on me. Another bright idea of Gruber's, I reckon. He had me figured for a Knights of Labor organizer, which suited me just fine, made good cover, threw him off the track. And I reckon he figured I couldn't do much organizin' in Wyomin' if I was wanted there for triple murder." Eyes fastened on Frank Gaylord over the cup's rim, he drank the coffee.

"Mr. Gruber," Swain said, "is a clever, dangerous, and ambitious man."

Morrell lowered the cup. "So is Gaylord," he said harshly.

"No," Frank Gaylord said. Suddenly he was very tired, because he knew all that Morrell spoke was truth. It added up, it had to. And, of course, he himself bore more guilt than he had dreamed of. "No," he said. "I ain't all that." He leaned wearily against the rock face. "I'm just a man that maybe wore a badge too long. Maybe it got a little too heavy for me to carry."

"They do that, sometimes," Morrell said quietly. "Well, what do you think, Gaylord? You size it up the way we see it?"

Gaylord looked keenly at Morrell. The Texan met his gaze steadily and unafraid, all mockery gone, and a grief that was genuine showing in his eyes. Slowly Gaylord nodded. "I never doubted all along," he said, "that Gruber had it done. And, yeah . . . I think it was the way you laid it out. Not you, but—" He looked out into the darkness, seemed to see the wink of brass tacks in a shotgun stock. "Lang. More than likely. All right, Morrell, you can put up that hardware."

Morrell hesitated only a second; then he holstered the gun with a motion so swift that Gaylord hardly saw it. "You'll want your own irons." He passed Gaylord's weapons to him.

"Very well, Sheriff," Lord Peter Swain said. "What do you intend to do?"

Gaylord slid his own Colt into its leather. "First, bring

up my horses," he answered. "Then we'll talk." He worked
his way back up the rock face in the dark. It was snowing
harder and bitterly cold. But, thinking of Tom Lang and
Ross Gruber, Gaylord did not feel the chill; rage was too
hot a fire within him.

———————————

A day had passed and still the storm had not abated.
The men and horses hunkered in the lee of the rock, leaving shelter only to seek more firewood, dividing for their
mounts the rations and grain that Gaylord had brought.

"First," Gaylord said when he'd brought back his
horses, "I want to know what your plans are, Lord Peter."

Swain frowned. "Originally, on Morrell's advice, I had
planned to wait at Ten Sleep until after your election. He
assured me Mr. Wallace would be elected sheriff—and
only then would it be safe for me to reveal my presence in
Colter County. Otherwise, Morrell thinks, my own life
would be in danger. That, certain of the law's coopera-
tion, afraid of what I'd find in an investigation of Chain
Ranch, Gruber wouldn't hesitate to do away with me
before I could confront him with what I have learned
about his operations. And Morrell had said I could count
on no help from you; indeed, perhaps just the opposite."

"All right," Morrell said. "I misjudged you, Gaylord—and you misjudged me."

Gaylord nodded. "But if you had protection from the
sheriff of Colter County, you'd go in and fire Gruber?"

"Yes. And ask you physically to oust him, if necessary.
But, of course, perhaps that will not be necessary now. I
assume you will arrest him for these despicable murders?"

Gaylord said harshly: "Yes. That's what I aim to do."
He looked out at the swirling snow, anticipation burning

in him like the glow of whiskey. "He's been riding high. Now he'll be brought low. No more Chain. No more power. And I'll see him and Lang swing for murder." He paused. "But we got to hurry. Because after the election I may not be sheriff anymore."

The other two looked at him. "We had it out," Gaylord said. "I was wrong about who pulled the trigger, but right about who gave the order. He knows I'm on to him and he knows what I'll do about it. I'm finished as Chain's candidate and, God knows, I don't expect the little ranchers to back me. So I'm a dead duck as of election day." He touched the badge pinned on his coat. "But I'll still be wearing this for four days more, and have the authority that goes with it. That ought to be time enough."

Morrell rolled a cigarette and stuck it in his mouth. "If you can get back in time. There'll be no travelin' through this blizzard. And even when it quits it'll be a good two days, and maybe more, back to Warshield. It'll be touch-and-go whether we make it before the polls close."

Gaylord turned on him. "We?"

"We," answered Lew Morrell. "I signed on to work for Lord Peter; he's bought my gun till this is over. Besides . . . Clint and Joey and Billy Dann were all my friends. Yeah, Gaylord, I got a piece of this, too."

Gaylord looked at him for a moment, then dug into his pocket. "Catch," he said, and something bright winked across the fire. Morrell nabbed it deftly and looked at the star in his upturned palm.

"I'm deputizing you, then," said Gaylord. "Raise your right hand."

Morrell's mouth twisted in a grin. "You're damn well told," he said, and did so. When he had pinned on the badge he said, "Now the only thing left to do is pray for this snow to stop."

But it did not; it blew all that afternoon and night. Gaylord tried to quench impatience, but it was futile. From now on every minute counted; he had to act while he still had his badge.

Only four more days, less—and then it would no longer be his. That seemed strange, unbelievable. He had worn one for so long; his whole life for twenty years had been built around a little piece of metal smaller than a playing card. An ounce or so of steel and silver; but carrying it took all a man's strength and will. Well, as he'd said, maybe he'd carried it too long, maybe it was too heavy for him; maybe he'd be better off without it.

From that, his mind slipped to Carla Doane. His loss of Florence no longer bothered him at all, but Carla was a different matter. Well, he was not fool enough to expect her to forgive him. Badge and woman both gone; he would end as he'd begun, a long time ago, with nothing. Fair payment for his own greed, his own blind ambition; and he would take his medicine. All he could do was wish her well, hope she eventually would find a man worthy of her. She'd had bad luck with men: first Linwood Doane, then Frank Gaylord. . . . Damn it, was it going to snow all month? As it was, they'd have to break trail all the way down the mountains; it would take a day just to get to Ten Sleep. . . . He rolled up in his blankets and tried to catch some sleep. Finally, after a restless half hour, it engulfed him.

It was still snowing in the morning, but not as hard. Now the flakes fell vertically, and the wind had died. Gaylord, staring at the sag-bellied sky, made his decision.

Time was running out. "We've got to move," he said in a voice that brooked no argument.

———————————

The snow was belly-deep to their mounts as they worked back through the woods to where the trail should be. Gaylord put his mountain-bred packhorse in the lead as they started down the slope, urging the lightly burdened, surefooted, and hill-wise animal along with a rope's end. Feeling its way cautiously, instinctively, it floundered through the high-piled white, breaking trail, with Gaylord following on the other mountain horse. That left fair footing for Morrell's and Swain's less adept mounts.

It was nerve-racking traveling. They were wholly dependent on the horse's senses; if it lost its way, made a mistake, it might lead all of them to disaster, over some dropoff masked by drift, maybe over the cliff itself when they were into the great gorge. But its highland shrewdness never played it false; it found the trail and kept to it.

Meanwhile, behind Gaylord, Morrell watched, as best he could in the dancing snowfall, the heights and outcrops ahead of them. It was barely possible that Gruber might have sent men after Gaylord; if so, the snow probably would have blocked them; still, Gaylord and the Texan both were old hands, neither inclined to take any chance that could be avoided. Swain brought up the rear, a superb, experienced horseman with years of youthful service in India behind him.

And so they plowed and labored down the Big Horns' western slope, foot by foot and yard by yard and mile by mile, down through the tremendous gorge of Ten Sleep

Canyon, an ice-draped, snow-piled world of white, the trail, steeply slanting, treacherous at every step. As they descended, the snow thinned a little and the drifts were not so deep, and now the going was faster. But already twilight fell; the journey had taken more than a day, and now there was only forty-eight hours until the polls would close in Colter County, and Gaylord—probably—would no longer be sheriff. Even he, though, was too cold and hungry and exhausted to feel impatience when at last they saw the lights of Ten Sleep ahead. All he wanted was a few hours of warmth and rest, with his belly full of coffee and hot food.

They warmed themselves at the potbellied stove in the cafe, wolfed enormous suppers; Gaylord revived. Now he felt the urgency again. While the others rested he found the blacksmith-livery man, reclaimed his sorrel, procured fresh mounts for Morrell and Swain. An hour later they were in the saddle again; the snow had stopped, and they made good time for a while along a well-defined wagon road through badlands, even in the dark.

Past midnight, Gaylord halted them; they slept for four hours in the shelter of a cutbank, then rode on. Down in the basin now, he knew this country perfectly, and he led them at a smart pace. Nevertheless, he always kept to cover, off the skyline, swinging in a circuitous route south of Chain; he dared meet no one who'd pass word to Gruber that they were coming in—Frank Gaylord, Lew Morrell, and a stranger with an English accent. Gruber, Gaylord knew, would not have been idle. He knew now that he had misjudged Frank Gaylord and overreached himself. And if he learned, as well, that Swain had come to search his books, call him to account, he would know he had only two choices: run or fight. And Gaylord knew that he would not run. He would not give up Chain Ranch, the source of all his power, that easily. He would kill Gaylord to keep it, and he would kill Swain—or anyone else who stood in his way. So as daylight faded Gaylord pulled up in a clump of willows by a stream, an hour out of Warshield. "We'll wait here awhile," he said.

"Why?" Swain was cold, tired, impatient for the comfort of town.

"Because," Gaylord said, "I don't know what's happened in Warshield since I've been gone, what Gruber's been up to. All I know is that we're not riding in until the town's gone to bed. Then we'll find a place to hide you until I know what my next move is."

"Hide me!" Swain was indignant. "Now, see here—"

"No, you see here!" Gaylord's voice was rough. He touched his badge. "Tomorrow is election day. After the polls close then, it's damned unlikely I'll still be wearing this. I got to use it while I can, and use it right. It's my last chance to legally bring Gruber in for Clint's murder. And when it comes to that, you're my ace in the hole; I'll see nothing happen to you. For God's sake, man, do you think Gruber'll stand still, without a fight, and let you strip him of his power? Until I can protect you, your life isn't worth a plugged nickel if Gruber finds out you're here. With you dead, your people in England would have to start all over again. You've got to lay low until I know what my next move is. I need information, I need a place to hide you, and I need men to help us. And there's only one place I can get all that."

"Where?" Swain asked.

Gaylord shifted in the saddle. "At the house of a woman named Carla Doane," he said.

Well after midnight they entered the town from its western outskirts, threading through its few back streets, dark now. Then, ahead, Gaylord saw it: the familiar outline, Carla's house. Something wrenched within him. How often had he approached it on the sly like this? . . . Then he pulled up his horse. A light still burned in the kitchen; she was up late. Then he eased. Of course she would be, the night before election day.

"Stay here," he told Morrell and Swain, leaving them in a pool of shadow. He dismounted, handed reins to Swain, and went forward on foot. He knew the way by heart, opening the back gate easily by feel; then through the well-kept yard and up the steps. Gently he rapped on the back door.

For a moment there was silence. Then the curtain over its glass panel was pulled back; Gaylord found himself staring into the face of Terry Fielding—and the muzzle of Fielding's gun. After a second Fielding recognized him. Slowly the door swung open. "All right, Gaylord," the lawyer said. "Come in." But he kept his snub-barreled Colt leveled.

Tieless, he was in his shirtsleeves, his face drawn and haggard. Then Carla whispered, "Frank—" Gaylord turned. She stood in the corner of the room, fully dressed, and she looked older, tired, eyes smudged with weariness—but to him she had never seemed lovelier. She took a step toward him, then halted.

Fielding said, "Did you get Morrell?"

"I got him, but he didn't kill Clint and Joey." Gaylord

spoke swiftly. "Listen, Terry, Carla, I got to have some help. . . ." He told them quickly about Morrell and Swain, and Fielding's jaw set. He lowered the gun. Gaylord finished: "Anyhow, I . . . I know the truth now. I know what a fool I've been, and . . . that don't matter. What matters is this: I've still got this badge, and as long as I'm wearing it I aim to use it. I want to get Swain out of sight, hide him here until you can find me a dozen men, two dozen, who want to help me get rid of Gruber. I'll deputize all of 'em and we'll ride for Chain and protect Swain while he fires Gruber. Then I'll arrest—"

"You'll arrest nobody," Terry Fielding said.

Gaylord stared at him. "What?"

"You aren't the sheriff of Colter County anymore," Fielding said. "You haven't been since the day you went to Chain, before you hit Morrell's trail."

"Wait a minute," Gaylord said.

"It's true, Frank." Carla came to him. "Remember, you weren't elected. You were hired by the county board, at Gruber's behest. Well, he had you fired by the county board, too. For malfeasance of duty, failure to stop the rustling. He took your badge away days ago and gave it to Tom Lang. Made Lang acting sheriff, called a new Republican convention, struck your name off all the tickets, put Lang's on with stickers. You are just an ordinary citizen now, and the word is that Gruber has signed a warrant against you for rustling. Lang has orders to arrest you if you show your face in town."

Gaylord drew in breath. "Well," he said. "Well . . ." His mind wrestled with the implications of this. Then he remembered Morrell and Swain out there in the darkness. "Terry," he said. "Tell 'em to come in, will you? If it's all right with Carla."

"It's all right with me," she said. "Terry, go ahead."

Fielding hesitated, then went out. Gaylord dropped into a chair. "So I don't have the badge any longer. Gruber's running Lang. Who're you running in Clint's place?"

"Nobody," she said. "We couldn't find anybody to run."

Suddenly Gaylord stood up. "What do you mean?"

"Terry wanted to, but I wouldn't let him. It would have been suicide." Carla's face worked. "As soon as Lang was appointed, he deputized a lot of Chain gunmen. They're all over town. Every time one of our people speaks up, he gets arrested—and then he gets beaten up. And I've had the word from Lang direct. Anybody we nominate is a dead man. Maybe it's true, maybe it isn't. All I know is that neither Terry nor I could take responsibility for asking anyone to run in the face of such a threat. And I wouldn't let Terry run himself."

"You wouldn't let— You and Terry are pretty close," Gaylord said. All at once he felt his fatigue. Before he could say anything else Morrell, Swain, and Fielding came in.

Carla looked nervously at Fielding. "Did you put the horses out of sight?"

"In the carriage house," Fielding said.

"This house is watched day and night, I'm almost sure of it," Carla said. Then she turned to Morrell. "Lew, I'm sorry if we thought harshly of you. Frank has told us—"

"It wasn't your fault. Carla Doane, meet Lord Peter Swain."

"Delighted," the Englishman said, and when she put out her hand he raised and kissed it. Carla looked surprised, then pleased. As Fielding made sure that all the blinds were down, she poured coffee from a big pot on the stove. "Anyhow, there it is," she said, as they drank it. "Gruber and Chain Ranch have clamped down an iron hand on this town. There'll be Chain gunmen watching the polling place tomorrow . . . Lang will be reelected without opposition. Then anybody who moves against Chain will be an outlaw."

Swain's face reddened. "I will not tolerate this. I will not have my ranch used for such purposes. I intend to confront this man Gruber and have it out with him!"

Fielding said quietly, "Don't be a fool, Lord Peter. The best thing you can do is slip out of here quietly now and go to Cheyenne. See the association people there and enlist their help. If you stay here, Gruber will see that you don't live long enough to fire him."

"I am sorry," Swain said. "That is not my way of doing business. I hired the man and I can let him go. And once he is gone, you are quite free to do with him what you like." He struck the table. "But I will not leave without a confrontation with that man!"

They all looked at him and recognized his purpose. "Then you'll have to hide here for a while," Fielding said. "Maybe a long while. Until the dust has settled and Gruber's off guard and maybe I can get some men together. Meanwhile, we've been euchred out. We've just all been euchred out."

His eyes ranged over Gaylord, Morrell, and Swain. "Frank, you and Lew had better ride out right away. There's still time. But you're finished here, both of you, until things change. . . ."

"No," Gaylord said.

"Frank." Carla came to him. "Please listen to Terry. I can't hide you all. You've—"

Gaylord stood up. "I don't want you to hide me, Carla,"

he said quietly. Slowly, carefully, he unpinned his badge. "All right," he said. "I don't own that anymore. Somehow, it makes it easier. In a way, it's always been bigger than I was; it's dragged me this way and that. It's kept me poor and it's kept me tired, trying to live up to it. And now it's off, and all at once I feel free. I'm not Sheriff Gaylord any longer. I'm just Frank Gaylord. For the first time since I was twenty."

"Frank." Carla's face was pale. "You're not making sense."

"To me I am," he said. "That badge, that hunk of tin. That goddamn piece of metal. In the long run, it's been a star I followed in the wrong direction. It's cost me everything I really ever wanted: it even"—his eyes met hers—"cost me you."

She opened her mouth to speak, but he went on.

"So I'm shut of it right now," he said. "I'm free at last to do what I want to do."

"Frank, no," said Carla. "You can't—"

"Yes, I can," Gaylord said. He saw how Swain was staring at him glazedly, nearly dead with fatigue. Before he went on, he lifted Swain by one arm and led him to Carla's bedroom. "I think you'd better lie down here," he said. "Later on I may need you."

"No," Swain murmured. But when he sprawled out on the bed he closed his eyes. Gaylord looked down at him, then went back to the kitchen. "Watch out for Swain," he said. "After I finish with Lang and Gruber, his decks will be clear. He's a good man, and he can put in a new administration at Chain that'll make everything different." Gaylord loosened his gun in his holster. "Where does Lang stay, now that he's sheriff?"

"I wouldn't tell you, Frank." Carla's voice was husky, frightened. "I love you too much."

"Love," he said. "Honey, you've put your bets on the wrong horse. I love you, too. I was off the track for a while, with Florence Gruber, but—but it doesn't matter now. I just want Lang, and then I want Gruber. Then we'll work it out."

"Gaylord, wait," said Fielding, but Gaylord shoved by him. "All right, I'll find him on my own," he said, and he stalked toward the front door. But before he reached it fists hammered on it. Then it suddenly broke open, flew inward, and all at once Tom Lang, carrying his shotgun, and Ross Gruber were there.

And at the same instant the back door opened and the man named Withers stood there with drawn gun.

CHAPTER XII

As the sawed-off shotgun centered on his belly, Frank Gaylord halted. "Stand fast," Tom Lang rasped.

Gaylord lifted his hand away from his gun.

Lang moved on down the corridor, skull-face grinning, pushing Gaylord ahead of him with the shotgun barrels. Gruber came close behind, Colt out, square face triumphant. "Frank," he said. "Did you really think we were that stupid? Not to watch this house day and night, knowing that you'd come here soon as you returned?" Then they were in the kitchen. Withers had already lifted Fielding's gun, and Lew Morrell, back against the wall, had his hands raised.

"Now, isn't this a pretty scene," Gruber said, as Lang stepped aside. "Rustlers and murderers and their fancy women all together. Sheriff Lang, you've made a big haul tonight. You've got Morrell, who killed the Wallaces. You've got former Sheriff Gaylord, who branded Chain Ranch cattle with his own brand, as we can prove to the association and the legislature. And you've got a woman of the town plying her trade—Mrs. Doane, I mean. I suppose Fielding was someone's accomplice."

Carefully, warily, still keeping his Colt aimed, he went to the stove and picked up the coffeepot. "Some, in the dead of night, we will take in. Others may stay here—dead. Morrell, for instance, who came back to his

inamorata, Mrs. Doane. And, finding her in bed with
Fielding, killed them both in a fit of jealousy. Or . . .
we'll work out something. Of course, Frank Gaylord goes
to Rawlins on a charge of rustling, and—" His brows
arched. "Does it surprise you, Frank, that I have a solu-
tion for every problem, an answer to every question?
Well, that's my specialty. I think ahead, work out these
situations in my mind. When Florence wrote me that she
was being run out of Philadelphia—she's not quite the
sweet little virgin, my dear sister, that we led you to
imagine—I immediately thought of how I could turn the
burden of her presence to my advantage."

He grinned. "I had you two paired before she even got
here. But, God, you bored her, Frank. She's used to a lot
more action than you provided. Lucky for her that Tom
Lang was around to fill in the gaps while you were
gone. . . ." Then he said, "Withers, I think you'd better
start collecting guns. Don't get in Tom's line of fire. These
people are tricky."

"Yes, sir." Withers approached Morrell, who stood with
hands high, back against the kitchen wall.

"A plan for every contingency," Gruber continued.
"Wallace fouled me up, but Tom took care of him—not
with his trademark, of course, the shotgun. And then you
wouldn't go along. That was my only misjudgment.
Usually I'm pretty accurate, but you foxed me. I didn't
quite have my hooks—or Florence's—in you quite
enough. But that's all right, I'll take care of that, too. And
if anybody comes from England to plague me, I've got
that arranged—"

"Indeed?" a cool voice said from the doorway connect-
ing the bedroom to the kitchen. "I think not, Major
Gruber. I can imagine no plan which will keep me from

discharging you from the management of Chain Ranch as of this moment."

———————————

Every head in the room jerked around then to stare at the wiry Englishman in the doorway, unarmed, yet impressive in his righteousness, as if his trust in law and rectitude were armor enough. Gruber's face turned the color of tallow. "You," he whispered, and the Colt in his hand sagged.

"Indeed," Lord Peter said again. "And—"

Gaylord heard no more. Because Lang was staring at Lord Peter, momentarily slack-jawed, and that shotgun had to be taken out; and then Gaylord left the floor in a long, swooping dive. Lang, aware of movement, squawked and whirled, but he was too late. Gaylord came in underneath the sawed-off barrels, knocked them up, and the room literally shook as both triggers went, eighteen buckshots slamming into the ceiling, bringing down a rain of plaster. Then Gaylord had wrenched the gun from Lang, his weight bearing the skull-faced man to the floor. Lang howled something, but Gaylord raised the shotgun high, and then, with all his strength, he brought the copper-studded stock smashing down. He felt bone give beneath the force and Lang was limp. Gaylord flung away the sawed-off and rolled. As he came up he was aware of more guns roaring: Morrell's drawn Colt lanced flame and Withers was knocked back across the table. His body hit the oil lamp there and it skittered to the floor, smashed, and spread a tongue of dancing flame. Gaylord clawed for his own gun, but too late. As Morrell turned, Gruber fired. Morrell staggered and dropped to one knee. Gaylord had a glimpse of Swain standing slack-jawed; then flame licked up the kitchen curtains with a hungry sound, behind Gruber's back. Gruber dodged aside, and Gaylord was reaching for his Colt when Fielding dodged across his field of fire. "Carla!" Fielding yelled, and seized her, pulling her sideways.

The house was pine, sundried, painted, and now flame spread across the floor at the base of the wall. Gruber turned and yelled, "Gaylord!" He raised his gun, then dodged again as burning curtains fell. Then Swain, coming out of his paralysis, launched himself at Gruber. Gruber saw him coming, stepped aside, nimble for so large a man, and slammed his Colt barrel against Swain's head. The Englishman went down. Fielding was dragging Carla toward the door. The whole east wall and the rear of the kitchen were in flames now. Gaylord, Colt out, felt the heat as he raised his gun.

Gruber was a flickering target in the orange light. He punched off a shot and Gaylord heard its mean whisper by his shoulder, and before he could fire, Gruber had jumped over Swain's prone form and was in the doorway to the bedroom. Gaylord loosed two slugs from the Colt, saw them plow splinters. They would drive Gruber back. Carla was safe; Fielding had her out. And beyond her he could think only of Gruber; Gruber was all he wanted. He ran for the doorway, thumbing back the hammer.

With sense enough to pivot as he hit it, he twisted his body sideways to make a smaller target. Gruber was in the corridor, and his shot sliced by Gaylord's belly. Gaylord fired at him and Gruber dodged, and then he was in the front hall, where stairs led to a part of the house Carla had not used since her husband's death. Gaylord heard Gruber's pounding footsteps on the stairs, heard behind him the roar of hungry flames devouring sundried boards.

That did not matter; nothing mattered except that he had
two more rounds in his gun and Gruber was up there
somewhere. And Gruber was the man he wanted, the man
he had to have. For Clint, for Joey, for Billy Dann and
Phil Hoff, and for everything he had cost Frank Gaylord.
Gaylord dodged to the foot of the stairs. Gruber fired
down at him. The bullet plucked Gaylord's arm, knocking
away skin and a quarter inch of meat. Gaylord went up
the stairs at a run. Gruber himself could not have more
than two rounds left. He saw Gruber's face, square, contorted, at the stair's head, halted, lined his Colt, and
Gruber dodged again behind a corridor, was in the up-
stairs hall now. Safe, and able to rake the stairs.

But now smoke from the fire boiled up them, a thick,
black, breath-sucking cloud. Gaylord laughed; under that
cover, he plunged upward. Now he was in the hall. Below,
there was a crackling, roaring sound. The corridor was
thick with smoke. Gaylord yelled: "Gruber!"

Then he heard glass smash. A draught of air cleared the
hall. He saw Gruber at the hall's end, hoisting a window,
stepping out onto the roof of the wing below. From there,
an easy drop to the ground, and Gruber would be in the
clear. Gaylord ran for him, but Gruber yelled something
and fired again, and Gaylord shrank back just in time.
Then Gruber was on the roof.

Gagging, coughing, in the smoke that filled the hall,
Gaylord ran to the window. Eyes watering, he reached
the open frame, sucking in gulps of air. His vision cleared.
Gruber was scrambling down the gently sloping roof of
the annex; from its edge it would be an easy leap to the
ground below. Instinctively Gaylord started to plunge
through the window, then halted. Familiar with the

layout of the house, he knew what was under that section of roof, and—

"Gruber!" he yelled.

Gruber heard his voice. Poised to jump, he turned and saw Gaylord in the window, outlined by flame behind him, a perfect target. In the flickering light, Gruber's face contorted, he took two long steps back in Gaylord's direction and raised his gun.

"Goddamn you!" he bellowed. "You have ruined me, ruined everything!" He aimed the Colt, mindless of his own safety, caught up in rage, bringing down the barrel exactly as if he were on an Army firing range. Gaylord brought up his own gun, eyes burning from the smoke. Gruber's shape danced, swirled in its blowing veil. Gaylord fired.

Gruber's shot went wild, delayed a fraction of a second too long. Gruber's right leg, bone smashed, went out from under him. He fell on the roof, but lifted himself with his arms. Then, directly in front of him, part of the roof gave way. For the part of the house it covered was the kitchen, where the fire had begun. Suddenly orange flames licked high in front of Gruber. Then more boards collapsed, more fire blossomed at his right.

Now the whole roof shook. Gruber's eyes were wide in the cruel orange light. Dragging his leg, he made for the edge of the roof, then was balked by more flame. Now he was on a burning island of wood above an inferno, and he turned back toward the window. "Gaylord!" he cried. "Gaylord, for God's sake, help!"

There was only one kind of help Gaylord could offer. Even as he raised his gun again, lined it as carefully as Gruber had, Gruber saw and understood. He froze, mouth open, skin already blistering; he did not move; dared not for fear that Frank Gaylord's bullet would miss.

Gaylord fired and Ross Gruber, shot through the head, fell forward.

His face had barely hit the surface of the roof before the whole house shuddered. Then boards, shingles, Gruber, and all disappeared into a roaring, hungry inferno that swirled up the house's flank, an orange mass of leaping flame.

Gaylord, motionless for long seconds, then felt the searing heat. The hall was clogged with smoke, the whole building shaking dangerously. He turned and ran down the hall. There was another window at its other end. Not only locked, it was nailed tightly shut. Gaylord smashed the glass with his gun and knocked out the wood framing. He raked his boot heel along the lower sash, then holstered the Colt. As he looked out he saw white faces in the yard, like scraps of torn paper, upturned, and bodies lying on the grass. Then there was no time to see more; he slid through the window. Jagged bits of glass cut his hands as he hung dangling from the frame, boots fifteen feet above the ground.

Smoke and flame roared out of the broken sash above his head. There was nothing for it; Gaylord let go and dropped. He hit hard, rolled, and felt something give in his ankle. Then hands seized him, were dragging him across the grass.

"Carla," he yelled, full of fear. His smoke-burned throat closed up, choked. "Carla," he whispered.

"I'm here, Frank." She was bending over him. "Are you all right? Oh, God, are you all right?"

"I'll make it," he managed in a whisper. "Swain? Where's Swain and Lew?"

Fielding, close by, said, "We got 'em out. Lew took a bullet, Swain's got a busted head, but they'll both live." He added sickly, "Lang and Withers are still in there."

"And Gruber," Gaylord husked.

"We saw," Fielding answered; and for a moment then there was nothing but the roaring of the fire. The whole house was going now, lighting the sky, and people yelled and a fire bell rang. But it was all right, because Carla was safe; and the others; nothing else but that was of any consequence.

Then, with Carla's help, Gaylord struggled to his feet. At a safe distance, they stood there, watching the building shake, then, wall by wall, collapse. "I'm sorry, Carla," Gaylord whispered, leaning on her.

Her arm was around his waist, and now it tightened. "It doesn't matter," she answered in a strange voice that carried above the roar of flames. He could not tell whether she was laughing or crying; she just held him desperately. "Let it burn! We'll build another one!"

We. Gaylord looked down at her, and he steadied himself on the one ankle that was not sprained, and as she leaned her head against his chest he stroked her hair. "Yeah," he said quietly. "You and me, we'll build another one." And he was still holding her in his arms when the fire brigade thundered, too late, into the yard.

CHAPTER XIII

"Sheriff," Callaway said. "Stage is ready to pull out."

Gaylord rose and went to his office door. Winter wind whipped dust along the street, ruffling the blond hair of the slender woman in traveling clothes being helped into the coach by the driver. Seated, Florence Gruber looked out the window, caught sight of Frank Gaylord standing there, and turned her head. There was something lonely and pathetic about her; and as the driver mounted the box Gaylord felt a thrust of pity. Then it faded. She was every bit as hardbitten as her brother. He had been present when she loosed her obscene tirade of hatred at Lord Peter Swain, who had brought her the news of Gruber's death—and at himself as well. Not even grief for Ross Gruber, but sheer ferocity at being cheated of the future she'd imagined. Gaylord's mouth thinned. She would get along, he thought. She was as hard as anyone he had ever met. Anywhere she landed, she would get along.

He watched the stage rattle down the street, turn east, and vanish. With it gone, he raked his eyes up and down the main street of Warshield. Nothing on it had altered in the past forty-eight hours, and yet it was a different town, he thought. The air had a different feel; there was no longer that tension like the pause before a storm: that storm had broken; now it was over.

Gaylord looked down at his chest and fingered the badge pinned there. He had not asked for it; they had forced it on him: Fielding, Carla, Swain—even Sir Randolph Hart, when he had learned the truth about Ross Gruber.

It was Fielding who had set the thing in motion, even before the embers of Carla's house were dark. In the doctor's office, where Swain's head and Morrell's smashed shoulder and Gaylord's sprained ankle were being bandaged, he said, "Well, the polls still open in three hours. And neither party has a candidate for sheriff."

Gaylord raised his head and looked at him.

"Frank," said Fielding, "I could get together a rump convention of both parties in about an hour. We could recertify you as a candidate. Put you back on the Republican ticket—and on our own as well." He smiled thinly. "In about an hour we could have some stickers printed with Gaylord's name on 'em. To go over Lang's and Clint's. What about it?"

Swain sipped the drink the doctor had given him. "I think I have a better offer for Mr. Gaylord. I'll be needing a new manager for Chain Ranch—a man of courage, ability, and integrity. I would like to offer Mr. Gaylord that position." He paused. "You'd have the same salary we were paying Gruber, plus the right to run stock on our range in your own name. And, eventually, I daresay it could lead to considerable future benefits. You would be, after all, a power in the government of this county and this territory."

Now Fielding and Swain both were staring at him. So was Carla, sitting across the room. Gaylord rose, limped to the window of the doctor's office, and looked out across the sleeping town. "Carla?" he said.

"The decision's yours to make, Frank. I don't care what it is, so long as you're happy."

Manager of Chain, Gaylord thought. And they would come to him—the others, the powers, like Shell, Sir Randolph Hart, MacAlpine . . . and Gruber's salary had surely been three times, maybe four, what the county paid its sheriff. With money like that he could make Carla comfortable, give her everything she deserved. . . .

"Frank," said Fielding. "Like Carla says, the choice is up to you. But no matter who runs Chain, good, bad, or indifferent, this county needs the law. If Clint was still alive, I'd say take Swain's offer. But Clint is dead, and . . . there's no one else but you."

His voice was earnest. "Even with Chain reformed, we're not out of the woods yet. The association's still in power in Cheyenne, the maverick law's still in force, there's got to be a strong man, a good man, behind that badge. . . . I know what you're thinking: as manager of Chain, maybe you could draw more water, change things quicker. But . . ."

"But those wolves in Cheyenne would eat me alive before I knew what happened." Gaylord turned, smiling wryly. "That it, Terry?"

"I didn't mean—"

"Well, you're right," Gaylord said. He drew in a deep breath. "I had my crack at it, I saw how it works. It's not something I know how to handle."

He paused. "But a badge. Yeah. Yeah, a badge is about my size." He faced Peter Swain. "I'm sorry, Swain. But I'm not a cowman anyhow. I never have been. And I'm too old to learn, now. I'd better stick to what I know I can do." He smiled at Fielding. "You need a sheriff," he said, "and if your people want me—why, I'll be proud to serve."

Fielding looked at him. "They'll want you," he said. "When I finish talkin' to 'em." Then he came alive, always the politician. "Good Lord, it's getting late. I've got a lot to do!" He hurried out.

When the door closed behind him Carla came to Gaylord and took his hand. "I'll make sure you get the women's vote," she said and laughed.

Swain finished his whiskey and stood up. "Well, he'll have the vote from Chain Ranch and Sir Randolph's place, I'll see to that. Frank, I wish— But perhaps it's just as well. I'll keep Lew here to advise me while I go through Gruber's accounts and get the picture; he'll be my second in command. Then, if he cares to stay on—"

"Not me," Morrell said. "I'll stay for a while, but then I'm headed back to Texas. Wyoming's either too damned cold or too damned hot for me."

Swain chuckled. "Then I suppose Martin Shell will recommend a manager." He was serious. "One thing is certain, Frank. You can be sure that Chain will cooperate with you—and the rest of the county—in every way. I'll give you my word on that. Now . . . I am no longer a young man and it's been an exhausting time. Lew, if you will find us a conveyance and someone to drive it, I should like to head straight for my ranch. There is still the sad news to convey to Miss Gruber—and much to do."

"I'll see to it," Morrell said, then he went out.

"Now," Carla said, "I think we'd better—" She broke off as, outside, on the main street, trumpets blared. Then she ran to the window. "Frank! Come here!"

He hobbled over and stared. There they came, marching down the center of the street in the cold light of false dawn—the Warshield Silver Cornet Band, with George Hayes, the town barber, in the lead, waving his baton. Trumpets, trombones, drums, and fifes, they shattered the early morning stillness with a thunderous rendition of "There'll Be a Hot Time In the Old Town Tonight."

And there was just enough light for Gaylord to read the crudely lettered signs held aloft by two small boys marching with them. GAYLORD FOR SHERIFF!

Carla laughed. "Terry didn't waste a second, did he?"

———————

And that was only the beginning, Gaylord remembered as the dust raised by the stage's passage settled. It was the biggest election day Warshield had ever seen. Fielding managed everything, spreading the news about Gruber, restoring voters' confidence in Frank Gaylord, overseeing the printing of the stickers and the voting. For the first time in Gaylord's political career, he was unanimously elected to public office without opposition or a dissenting vote.

He closed the door, turned back inside the office, poured himself a cup of coffee, and drank it. Then he put on his coat and adjusted his gun in its holster. Last night the county board, apologetic, had sworn him back in. And then there had been another ceremony, presided over by Judge Merkel.

It was the first time, too, that Gaylord had ever celebrated his reelection by getting married.

He grinned. Carla was busy even now in the small house across town which they had rented until the big one could be rebuilt. He hungered for the sight and feel of her, but that, like their honeymoon, would have to wait. After all, he was on duty now.

He turned to Callaway. "Tom, you hold things down here. I'll go out and take a look around the town."

Callaway nodded, and Gaylord stepped out onto the sidewalk. The wind from the Big Horns was clean and cold. He drew in a deep breath of it, made sure the star on his sheepskin coat was tightly fastened, and, limping slightly, set out, as was his custom, on his routine ten o'clock patrol.